THEIR PRINCESS

HER ROYAL HAREM: LILY
BOOK THREE

CATHERINE BANKS

TURBO KITTEN INDUSTRIES

To Avery for his support and love.

ONE

Three large demon portals made of thick, swirling black smoke appeared in the center of the city park. Hundreds of fighters from the werewolf, mage, dragon, hybrid, and elf clans surrounded the portal, some shifted, some with weapons, and all on high alert.

Tensions ran high as we waited for the enemy to come out of the portal, to begin this war that we had tried so hard to avoid and dreaded for so long. This is where it would all be decided. This is where the battle for the worlds would end.

From the center portal, the Grand Advisor with a strange staff walked out with Jolmach, King of the Demons at his side. Behind them a wooden cart pulled by two oxen-looking demons carrying my parents, bound in chains, were the first ones to exit from the demon world.

My eyes focused on King Jolmach, Jol as I called him. He wore his full armor, his helmet covering his face and blocking his eyes from me, but I could tell he was not the Jol I had known during my stay. The Grand Advisor had brainwashed him once again and he would not view me as the friend that I was right now. I dreaded facing off against him during this battle. If he hurt me seriously, he would not forgive himself, and I didn't want to hurt him either, which would make for an intense and difficult fight.

The humanoid demon fighters that had been the hardest to fight last time we had faced them exited two by two out of the side portals. I realized then that they were the members of Jol's Council. The ones I had spoken to when I had met the Grand Advisor. That all felt like a hundred years ago now.

Five bull-headed demons walked out of the center portal behind Jol and the Grand Advisor, stationing themselves behind them with their axes in their hands, a ready expression on their faces.

Those on our side tensed and waited anxiously for what was to come. Would there be a battle, bloodshed, and possibly death? Or could I still prevent it somehow?

Leona whistled high and loud, the note making me, and most nearby, cringe. Once it ended, the Grand Advisor's fake appearance disappeared and his true one remained.

I stood alone, front and center, waiting to speak on our behalf and to try to prevent what had been foreseen. Especially the most recent one I'd had. Mason flew overhead, but quickly landed on my shoulder, tensed and ready to protect me if necessary.

Grandpa Nico, King of the Mages, teleported next to me, his staff in his hand. "Greetings, you must be one of my long lost brothers," he said to the Grand Advisor in a pleasant tone.

The Grand Advisor scowled. "What are you talking about?"

Jol turned to look at the Grand Advisor and growled. "What is this? Where are your horns?"

"He has none," I announced. "Because he is not a demon. This is his true form."

The Grand Advisor's eyes widened when he realized what had happened. "Will you remove my curse, or shall I remove your parents' heads?" he asked me.

Every single one of our fighters growled at the threat against my parents, myself included.

"You would be wise not to threaten them when surrounded by their family and clan," I said, and started forward. "I will remove your curse, if you agree to release my parents."

"I am a man of my word," he said.

That was a lie that I didn't even need to feel or smell to know.

"I will come forward to remove the curse," I said. "I must be near you to do it. Plus, I want to confirm the two in the cart are actually my parents and not a trick."

He waved at me like a bored king. "Come. Let's get this over with."

I looked at Jol, but he was focused on Grandpa Nico. Why wouldn't he even look at me?

It was likely because he realized that Grandpa Nico was the larger threat, which both irritated and made sense to me.

As I approached the cart, I realized there was another person inside, laying on their back ... Talrinir. She was unconscious and I worried dead, but I couldn't run to check on her.

"Dad?" I asked both mentally and aloud.

"It's me and your mother," he responded mentally and aloud as well.

Our mental connection wasn't very strong, but since I was part of the hybrids, it did exist.

Mom looked towards me and nodded once to let me know she was okay, even though they had a gag in her mouth. It made sense, since she was part siren. But, so was Dad, or did they not know that?

"The woman in the cart?" I asked mentally to Dad.

"Alive, but sedated."

"She's a friend."

"Understood," he replied and dipped his head once.

"The pup?"

"At the castle. Locked up," Mom replied.

"Are you satisfied?" the Grand Advisor asked, sounding irritated by my delay.

Why would he have left Dhun locked up at the castle? Was he afraid he would help us somehow? He was only one hellhound after all, albeit a tenacious little pup, but still.

I turned and looked at Jol again, but he was still solely focused on Grandpa Nico.

"Yes," I said. "Now, I will remove your curse." Striding forward, I released my powers, allowing the shadow snake out.

She slid along my shoulders, her tongue darting out to test the air for magic and potential threats.

Our thoughts were fully focused on the Grand Advisor and my plan.

If this didn't work, we would have to go with one of our

other backup plans. Some of them I was really, really hoping to avoid using as they meant things had gotten very screwed up.

Standing before the Grand Advisor, I didn't miss the sneer he gave before going back to scowling. He was convinced he was winning already. I didn't like that. I didn't like that one bit.

"Here is the promised mana stone with my magic in it," I said, and held it out.

He held out his open palm and I dropped it in it. A wide smile crossed his face as he gripped it tight, but then he smoothed his features out so quickly I thought I might have imagined it.

"To remove the curse, the snake has to bite you, so please stay still," I said calmly as the shadow snake flared her hood and hissed, showing off a bit.

He dipped his head. "I shall stay still."

"Withdraw," I ordered her. Subconsciously, I made sure to order that she only withdraw the pain curse and left the infection curse as it was.

She struck immediately, biting into the side of his neck, and removed the tiny bit of shadow power that was the pain curse. Done, she released her hold and moved back to my shoulders.

The Grand Advisor sagged forward, gasping in a shuddering breath, then straightened with a smile. "The pain is gone! Finally!"

With a deep breath, I drew Mason's sword from where it was hidden on my back, and swung it with all my might, the blade arcing to slice his head from his neck.

Before my blade could find purchase, my vision went dark and when I blinked again, I was on my back. Jol stood over me, his foot on my chest and club hovering above my head. Dad had a sword at Jol's neck and Zoman had a sword at Dad's neck.

"How disappointing," the Grand Advisor said with a deep sigh. "I thought perhaps we could come to some peaceful resolution, but clearly I was mistaken."

"You *are* mistaken," I wheezed. "You have used your powers, your hybrid siren powers of this world, to take over a world that is not yours, to manipulate and brainwash the demons. As Princess of the Hybrids and Demons, I will remove you from my peoples' worlds permanently. That is the only resolution in your future." Softening my voice I said, "Jol, look at me. Jol, you can break his hold over you. You can remove the mind-altering spell the Grand Advisor placed in your brain."

Jol's eyes moved down until they met mine, though his head did not move, and he said, "He has opened my mind, shown me how you have manipulated us. *You* are the enemy."

"You are sworn to protect the royal bloodline!" I snapped. "I am Princess Liliana Rubyserpent, a descendent of Third to Reign. I am your royal princess. You are sworn to protect me. Now, remove your foot and set aside your club!"

Jol scowled a moment, my words registering with the vow, connecting with the part of him that even the Grand Advisor's brainwashing could not touch.

The shadow snake appeared, flared her hood, and hissed

at him. Dark shadows spread from me, covering the ground beneath me, Jol, Zoman, and Dad.

Zoman's eyes widened and he took a hesitant step back.

Jol's eyes pinched in pain and he put a hand to his head before stumbling back several steps away from me, his club lowered.

"Do not listen to her!" Grand Advisor yelled and started to whistle.

Dad grabbed me and teleported us next to Grandpa Nico, who stood beside Mom and Talrinir, who was, thankfully, looking well except for a bump on her head.

Talrinir hugged me and I hugged her back. "I'm sorry you were hurt because of me," I whispered, but the Grand Advisor's whistle grew louder and caused extreme pain that made me clutch my head.

His whistle was cut off as Dad, Nana Jolie, and Great Aunt Leona all began to sing the same song, their voices carrying over the entire field.

Goosebumps broke out all over my body at their beautiful and terrifying song. Images began to flit across my vision. Images of the demons uniting with those of our world, all of us living happily together, while the Grand Advisor was chained and killed.

Dad's voice grew louder and a new vision played, one of Jol and I wearing crowns and standing before happy and healthy demons at houses in a dark forest, houses built by the hybrids.

"No!" Grand Advisor screamed and shattered the visions.

It was too late, though. Jol was free of the Grand Advisor's hold. He roared and shook his head. "How dare you! You used us! Manipulated us!"

The Grand Advisor backpedaled, heading at an angle away from the portals. "I protected you! Your land was ravaged, dead, and your people on the verge of extinction!"

"Lies!" I shouted. "You destroyed the land to coincide with your lies, with the diatribe you were spewing to make yourself seem important."

"There is a section of the land, hidden by wards, that is thriving. Your land isn't dead or dying. We can help you revive it," Dad announced.

"I already started! I brought two plants to life with just a bit of water and sunlight," I added.

"You are hereby banished from the demon world and your title is removed!" Jol bellowed.

A bright red burst of magic surged out of one of the portals and hit the Grand Advisor in the chest. He gasped and clutched at the spot, mouth opening and closing like a fish out of water as he tried to breathe.

Dad and Grandpa Nico teleported next to the Grand Advisor, coordinating their attacks against him. Their magic and weapons flashed.

Somehow, even weakened and open as he was, he managed to block and defend himself.

"Lily," Jol called as he walked to me.

I smiled at him. "Welcome back, Jol."

He dropped to a knee before me and bowed his head. "Thank you. You have saved us."

"It's not over yet," I said, and tapped his shoulder. "Stop bowing. We're equals. Plus, we need you on your feet and ready to fight."

Jol stood and shook his head. "He's lost. There will be no battle now."

"No," I argued. "My Nana and I have seen visions. This fight is not yet over. He still has some tricks up his sleeve."

"I will protect you," he said, watching the Grand Advisor and my dad fighting.

"*We* will protect her," Mason said as he, Kayden, and Trey joined us. "You need to be ready to hold your people back."

"What visions did you have?" Jol asked.

"You trying to kill me," I answered. "Many demons trying to kill my mates."

His eyes widened, then he frowned and said, "Well, I did try to kill you earlier, so perhaps –"

I shook my head. "That was not the fight I saw in my vision."

The Grand Advisor stumbled as Dad and Grandpa Nico continued attacking and pursuing him, then fell through a black smoke portal on the ground.

We all spun around, searching for where he had teleported to.

He stepped out of the portal beside us and whispered in Jol's ear.

Jol's body froze, his head tipped back, and he let out a long and loud whistle.

"Shit," I whispered. "He's calling the demons through the portal." I wasn't entirely sure how I knew, but I just ... did. "They're coming!" I shouted to those nearby. "Try not to kill them!"

Hundreds of demons of every kind poured out of the portals. Flying, crawling, humanoid, giant, and many types I had never seen even while in the demon world.

Most turned their eyes towards us and I knew this was my vision.

"They're coming after you three," I said. "Nana! My vision!"

"Protect Lily's mates!" Nana Jolie yelled and teleported next to us.

Grandpa Nico, Mom, and Dad teleported over as well. Grandpa Nico put a translucent bubble shield around us.

"What vision?" Dad asked.

Mom wrapped her arms around me, hugging me tight. "I'm so glad you're safe."

"Not for long," I whispered.

Nana Jolie explained the two visions we'd had, which made Mom and Dad both scowl.

"Differing visions is concerning," Mom whispered.

"There's more," I said and told them about Molly's drawings and visions.

"It's extremely concerning," Dad muttered.

"I think all of the visions will come to pass," I explained. "Or I'm seeing this vision while Nana is seeing a different one or something like that."

The demons crashed into our shield, but none were as aggressive as Jol. His club slammed into the shield and I felt the ground shake beneath us.

"Shit, he's strong," Grandpa Nico muttered.

"You have no idea," Dad grumbled and rotated his shoulder. "Pretty sure I've got a permanent click in this shoulder now."

"Please don't kill him," I begged everyone. "He's brainwashed. Normally, he's a really nice being."

"She's right," Mom agreed. "He's incredibly kind and just wants what's best for his people."

"Caleb!" Grandpa Nico grunted as the demons swarmed all over the top of the shield while Jol continued to hit it.

Dad added his own shield just inside of Grandpa Nico's, reinforcing it in case Grandpa's fell.

"I have to go out there," I said. "This is my vision and I have seen what happens." Or this was one of the visions Molly had had, which was more concerning to think about.

Taking a warrior shift, I ensured my body was covered in scales to protect me and drew on my mates' powers to give my hands claws. I also added the smoke scales, just in case.

"No," Trey growled.

I went up on my tip toes and kissed him lightly on the lips. "Love you."

Before anyone could protest or stop me, I ran out of the shield, straight into Jol, who was arched back to swing again. I knocked him away from the shield and back towards the portal.

"Jol, you have to stop this. We are not your enemy! I'm one of you," I said as I ducked his punches and jumped out of the way of his giant club. Growling, I punched him in the leg, smiling slightly when his bone cracked and he dropped to one knee.

I knew it wouldn't keep him down though, Jol would heal quickly.

"You are the enemy!" the Grand Advisor yelled. "You have betrayed your people by siding with the ones here. You want to eradicate the demons as proven by you mating the famed demon hunters."

"Shut up," I snapped at him. "I don't know how you're doing this, but I'm going to end you. I'm going to destroy you."

Before I could even take a step towards the Grand Advisor, Jol grabbed my hair and flung me backwards with it.

I landed on my back with an oomph, all of my air whooshed out of my lungs as his club struck my chest.

Shit. This was one of Molly's visions.

I tried to take a breath and winced. He'd broken at least two of my ribs. Crap.

Rolling over, I started to crawl towards the portal. Maybe if I could get Jol back into the demon world it would reset the Grand Advisor's brainwashing.

Someone scooped me up just as Jol was about to crush me with the club again.

"You trying to die?" my brother, Tony, asked. He was in his werewolf warrior shift so his words were a little slurred from talking with a wolf head.

"Through the portal," I ordered him as I gasped for breath.

He sighed. "I hope you know what you're doing because your mates are going absolutely insane inside of the shield and trying to fight our family to get to you."

Jol swung his club down and Tony dodged out of the way, growling at Jol.

We ran through the portal and he had to slide to a stop as we came face to face with a huge group of demons.

"Shit," he muttered and spun to the right as Jol followed after us.

"Jol! Please listen to me," I begged. "You are bound to *protect* me!"

"Lies!" he shouted and rammed into us with his shoulder, causing Tony to drop me.

I summoned my snake and she struck, biting into Jol's neck.

He fell to his knees and his head dropped forward.

"What are you doing?" Tony asked.

"I'm not sure," I admitted. "The power did it on its own."

"Princess," Azgon yelled as she ran towards me. She puffed up and hissed at the demons who had started to move closer to us.

"Azgon," I gasped and hugged her.

She stiffened in my hold at first and then patted my back in return. "The brainwashing is bad!" she shouted as we separated. "All the males are infected!"

"I need you to do me a favor," I said.

She nodded. "Okay. Okay."

"Go to the castle and free Dhun."

"The hellhound pup?"

I nodded. "They've locked him up and I think there's a reason. Please, go release him and lead him to the portals here."

She nodded. "You got it! Oh, watch out!"

Turning, we found Jol back on his feet and my shadow snake gone.

"Jol?" I asked. "Are you still feeling murder-y or are we friends again?"

He rubbed his head and groaned. "My skull feels like it's going to explode."

"Brainwashing does that to you," I said with a nod.

He looked at Tony and asked, "Who are you? You look like the hybrid king."

"This is Tony, my brother, Prince of the Hybrids, biological son of the king and queen," I introduced.

Tony dipped his head. "It's an honor to meet you, Demon King Jolmach."

"What's going on, little queen?" He looked at the portals and the gathered demons. "Fill me in, fast."

Fast was subjective, but I did my best to give him the shortened version.

When I finished, he pulled me into a hug and said, "I'm so sorry I hurt you."

I patted his back. "It's okay, I'm healed again. I'm sorry about your leg."

He stepped back and said, "I'm healed again already. So, all is well"

"Wait, you know how to defeat the Grand Advisor?" Tony asked. "Why haven't you done it yet?"

"Because we have to get through all of the visions first," I explained. "If I try to do it too soon, it might not actually be the way to defeat him."

At least, that's what I thought.

Jol turned to face the demons gathered and announced, "From now on, you obey Princess Liliana! Do you understand?"

They roared, chittered, and yipped their agreement.

Jol looked at me and said, "Lead the way, Demon Princess."

THREE

We stepped through the portal, a dozen demons at our backs, all ready to fight at my command, and headed towards the Grand Advisor.

He had several demons, mostly the generals, around him in a protective circle. As we moved closer, they parted, allowing us to see it wasn't just the Grand Advisor they were encircling.

I immediately froze as fear coursed through me at the sight of Mason, Kayden, and Trey kneeling on the ground with their hands bound in strange chains. The vision. This was another vision.

As soon as I moved towards them, the Grand Advisor snapped his fingers with a gleeful smile on his stupid, arrogant face.

My mates threw back their heads as they screamed in simultaneous agony.

Their pain transferred to me. Lightning coursed through

my veins, just beneath my skin, and I screamed with them, dropping to one knee.

"Lily!" Tony shouted and picked me up in his arms. "What's wrong?"

Jol stepped forward, putting his body between me and the Grand Advisor, his club in his hand.

The pain ebbed, allowing me to speak. "Their. Pain," I panted. "It transferred to me for a moment." I patted Tony's arm. "Set me down, Brother. I'm fine now."

He obeyed, but hovered close by. "What are we going to do about them?"

"Make your choice, Princess Liliana. Your mates' lives or your world, which will you choose?" the Grand Advisor sneered, standing behind them with a sword as though he were to be victorious.

He snapped his fingers again, the pain searing through them and our bond, making the four of us scream.

Jol charged at the Grand Advisor, roaring, but with a single loud, note, he caused Jol to still.

How was he able to effect Jol so quickly? Was it because he had been toying with his mind for so long?

It infuriated me immensely. I wanted to sever the connection as thoroughly as possible, to ensure he could never hurt Jol again.

"Make your choice, Liliana, or I shall kill your mates and this demon you seem to harbor feelings for!" Grand Advisor bellowed, his face reddening in fury.

My mind raced; how could I free them? How did this vision play out? What was I supposed to do?

But, from the farthest portal, I saw him and knew, deep

within my heart, I knew, that it was not me who was supposed to do anything. It was Dhun! My precious little, now somehow incredibly large, hellhound friend.

"Your mates or your world?!" Grand Advisor shouted.

"You shall have neither!" I shouted with a wide smile on my face.

He did not see the angry hellhound as he leapt through the farthest portal, making his way towards us, at the back of the Grand Advisor. His spines were puffed, but he did not rattle them as he moved silently closer, stalking. His jaws dripped with drool as he opened his mouth, fangs bared, and leapt onto the Grand Advisor.

Mom created a large portal beneath my mates' knees, causing them to fall through and land next to me.

Jol quickly removed their restraints, and they thanked him breathlessly.

Had we not still been in jeopardy, I would have made a joke about him being their handsome savior.

Dhun had inflicted a major wound on the Grand Advisor, but the generals began attacking him, forcing him to turn on them instead.

Jol rushed over, assisting the hellhound and incapacitating the generals quickly.

"Are you injured?" Trey asked as they stepped up to stand at my back.

I looked over my shoulder at them and smiled. "I'm fine, handsome."

Kayden dropped his forehead to rest on my shoulder and exhaled. "Thank goodness."

"This vision is almost over," I whispered. "I'm not certain what will come next."

Just as Jol was about to take out the Grand Advisor, his hands wrapped around his throat, the scene shifted.

Mom and Dad suddenly stood on either side of me, deep frowns on their faces as they explained they had seen one of the other visions.

"Which means we're nearing the end," I said and exhaled a relieved breath.

"None of this makes sense," Dad muttered. "How is he doing this when he's been weakened in each of the different instances? He must have help. It must be someone else helping him."

"Leona is searching with Jolie to try to find them," Mom said. "We all sensed that we were missing something."

"I've never heard of a power like this, neither had Grandpa Dalton," Dad whispered.

Great Grandpa Dalton was Jolie's father, former King of the Sirens. If he'd never heard of this power, then it must be due to ...

"It's likely because he's a hybrid," Mom said, finishing my thought for me.

"We really are terrifying," I whispered.

Mom and Dad didn't disagree with me.

"I'm going to go talk to Mom," Dad said and teleported away.

"I'm going to check on Leona," Mom said and created a portal at her feet, falling through it.

Mason, Trey, and Kayden suddenly each put a hand on

me. Mason on my arm, Kayden on my shoulder, and Trey on my hip.

Looking back at them, I saw their eyes focused on something and turned in that direction.

Liam headed towards us, an unconscious Maya in his arms.

Simultaneously, fury consumed me, along with worry for my friend.

"What are you doing?" I demanded and took a step forward.

He smirked and said, "I told you I would test out your little friend here. So, what will it be, Lily? Your friend or the demon world? You must choose."

My eyes widened and my mouth dropped open. "You're working with the Grand Advisor?"

Shrugging, he said, "I was never going to hold a powerful position here, but with him, I will."

Of course the Grand Advisor had found people like him, weak idiots who wanted power and would give up our world for it.

"I'm going to skin you with my teeth," I hissed, my tongue coming out forked and my fangs elongating even though I stayed in my human form.

He flinched back, fear on his face.

Good, he should know I was to be feared. He should know never to touch my friends, especially not my best friend!

"Put her down this instant or I'll hold you down while she tears your skin from your muscles," Mason threatened in a flat, serious tone.

My lower body tightened, and I knew my mates could scent my arousal, but I didn't care. Yes, that was hot!

"Fuck off, bird brain," Liam snapped.

Jaeden ran from behind us, ram horns atop his head, and slammed into the side of Liam, knocking Liam and Maya to the ground.

I moved forward to help, but Kayden's grip tightened.

Tony, the elf, and my brother Tony suddenly appeared, dropping down next to Jaeden to help beat the shit out of Liam, who never stood a chance.

My brother let elf Tony get the last hit against Liam while he picked up Maya.

"We've got her, Lily. You focus on the battle," my brother said.

Exhaling, my shoulder dropping a bit, I said, "You three should take her away from the battlefield. I'm not sure what he did to make her unconscious like she is."

Jaeden set his hand on her face and nodded. "She's a bit feverish, so probably a potion. Let's go."

FOUR

The Grand Advisor stood just before the portals, blood dripping down his face and his left arm. "You are a troublesome lot. Brayden and Klaus were right."

"So, you admit that you are a sibling of Grandpa Nico's?" I asked calmly.

"Please, you'd figured that out long ago," he said and waved his hand dismissively. "Your parents are powerful, but your power comes from your innocent appearance. I thought you were a gullible, spoiled princess." He scoffed. "How shallow of me."

I smiled. "Yes, that was very shallow of you. What is your name?"

"Why?"

"Well, I've always felt weird calling you 'Grand Advisor.' I was hoping now you'd finally give us your real name."

"You can call me, 'Your Majesty,'" he sneered.

I rolled my eyes. "I don't even call my parents that. Please, get over yourself. You're not that special."

His brows furrowed. "I shall enjoy cutting your head from your body and displaying it from the castle."

My mates growled.

Smiling, I said, "You can try, John."

His furrowed brows loosened a second before furrowing again. "John?"

"You won't give me your name, so I figured it must be a basic name, like John." I shrugged. "Seems fitting."

He snarled and magic crackled around his body. "My name is Valentino and soon you will all refer to me as King Valentino!" He weaved a pattern with his hands, a movement I hadn't ever seen done before. "Good thing I've still got an ace up my sleeve or all of these years of work dealing with the pitiful demons would have been for naught." He pulled out the stone I'd given him with my magic and drew it out, absorbing it into his body.

Despite knowing that the magic had a curse within it that would eventually weaken him, I was scared because I didn't know how long the curse would take to go into effect.

"Ready?" Kayden asked calmly behind me and used his thumbs to dig into a knot on my upper shoulder.

I nodded once. "Ready."

The worst part was waiting for Valentino to make his move first. I hated waiting.

Trey reached over and squeezed my hand. "Patience, Princess. I know that's something you've never excelled at."

"Waiting sucks," I whispered.

"Good things come to those who wait, or at least that's what your parents always told us," Mason muttered.

"Any word on the other siren?" I asked.

Dad teleported next to me and whispered, "Leona's found the accomplice, a siren like you thought. We're going to wait until they make their next move before attacking."

I nodded. "Understood."

He teleported away again.

"I need that power," I whispered.

"No, then we would never find you," Mason grumbled. "You'd teleport all over to visit people and places and it'd be like finding a needle in a haystack."

Kayden sighed softly. "Don't even mention her having that kind of ability, it stresses me out thinking about it."

Rolling my eyes was the only response they got out of me.

Dhun and Jol jogged up to us from behind and I bent over to hug Dhun. "You're even bigger than when I last saw you!"

He yipped and his tongue lolled out of his mouth.

"He won't stop growing for at least a year," Jol explained. "He's actually quite large already for a hound, so I think he's going to be the largest one yet."

"Probably Lily's fault," Kayden whispered.

I elbowed him in the stomach. "Rude!"

All of the men laughed, including Dhun.

"I'm weaving your deaths and you're chattering and laughing?" Valentino asked, his hands still moving through the air, reminding me of martial arts movements my grandpas practiced sometimes. Though, their practice of those movements was for calming and centering yourself, which I highly doubted was Valentino's plan.

"It's hard to take someone playing with the wind seriously," I said and shrugged, acting unconcerned despite the fear coursing through me. I had to believe that the visions were true and we would win. I had to. The moon rose closer to its zenith and I knew the time was coming. The time for the prophecy to be enacted.

"Laura! Now!" Valentino screamed.

Laura? Laura must be his siren accomplice.

I turned to look behind me, in the direction he'd looked, but a wave of magic, reminiscent of being hit by a wave of water, slammed into me from both sides simultaneously.

My breath was taken and I felt like I fell through the ground and into an ocean of water. Darkness clouded over my eyes a moment, until I heard Great Aunt Leona and Nana Jolie singing. Their song pulled me to the surface and I drew in a deep, long breath, my lungs burning with the precious air.

Dad knelt beside me, a hand on my back and asked, "Are you alright, cub?"

Nodding, I climbed to my feet. All of my mates were getting to their feet as well as Dhun and Jol. "You got her?" I guessed.

Dad nodded. "Leona took care of them."

Valentino stood before us, a dark magic like black oil spinning around his feet and taking over his eyes. "So troublesome."

Closing my eyes, I summoned my shadow snake. "Activate Goddess Mode."

Intense warmth from my chest spread throughout my body, increasing in heat until I felt like it was pouring out of my skin. Scales formed from my neck down to my toes, a tail grew from my lower back, my tongue grew longer and forked, scales lined my temple, and I felt my eyes shifting. Magic swirled withing my body and around me, creating a slight dust cyclone around my feet. Memories of my ancestors, those who had this power before me, flitted across my closed eyelids, giving me insight, tips, and a history of who I really was. My head fell back as I accepted this power fully, accepted who I was. I would take on any enemy of the demons or hybrids. I knew ... I *knew* I would defeat Valentino now. I would finish what my great grandmother had started. However, I also knew now that there would be a sacrifice. Using this power didn't just use your power and weaken you, it consumed part of your power. It would permanently erase part of my power, destroy the connection I'd just had with my ancestors, and I could never restore it.

It was the only way.

I was Liliana, a demon and hybrid shifter, the royal from both worlds, and it was time for me to protect my people.

Opening my eyes, I smiled at my mates, who stared at me in awe.

Kayden snapped a picture on his cell phone.

Turning to my adoptive parents, I said, "My ancestors thank you for protecting and raising me so well."

Mom and Dad's eyes widened, but the most shocked was me as they both bowed their heads. Mom said, "It was our pleasure."

"Jol," I called and held out my right hand. "It's time for you to take my hand, accept our agreement, and become an ally to my world."

Jol, without missing a beat, took my hand, and said, "Yes, Goddess Liliana of the Demons."

Facing Valentino, I saw the fear on his face and smiled. "My great grandmother tried to give you a second chance, but you've spit on that and now, you shall be punished."

Dark power swirled within Jol and at the point of our joined hands, both of our powers began to merge. His eyes glowed red, his horns grew thicker and longer, and he roared his rage. A rage I felt within me as well.

The power grew greater within me. It was like Jol was a conduit to all of the demons and the demon world, drawing more and more into me.

It was so much. Almost too much. If I didn't use it soon, I worried I might explode, though I wasn't sure it would be a good explosion like when I accepted the shadow powers. My power, a piece of myself deep within my core, sizzled hot, ready to be used.

"Valentino, you committed grave sins, murdered inno-cents, and all for an attempted coup. You are hereby sentenced to death. Goodbye." Inhaling, I gathered the power between Jol and I, forming it into a basketball sized ball, and shot it straight into Valentino's chest.

The cursed power I'd given him had started working, making him stagger just before the power hit him, preventing him from teleporting to safety.

The ball of power hit him, his body lifted up off the ground, a scream tore from his throat, and then ... he disap-peared. Completely disintegrated. The power that was left exploded out, sending a wave outward, but somehow didn't harm anyone it touched. In fact, the demons smiled when it touched them.

At the spot Valentino had been, a bright white light

glowed, and a silver lily grew up from the ground, the tips red like they'd been dipped in blood.

The prophecy had been fulfilled.

The three large portals to the demon world had disappeared, along with Valentino.

The power within me burned hot, like a wound being cauterized, making me wince.

Turning to face the demons and those of my parents' world, Jol and I, hand-in-hand, raised our joined hands, and I announced, "The war is over!"

FIVE

The crowd erupted in cheers and screams as I fell to my knees, my magic beyond expended. I started to fall to my back, but Jol caught me with an arm around my upper back.

"Well done, Goddess," he whispered.

"Not so bad yourself, King Jolmach," I whispered back, smiling as much as I could. It had been a long time since I'd felt so utterly exhausted and weak. In fact, I couldn't feel my magic ... at all. "Why aren't you exhausted?" I asked, trying to distract myself.

"Because you simply took magic from me and others. I was just a conduit," he explained.

Mom scooped me out of Jol's arms, hugged me to her chest, and sobbed loudly. "Lily! You did it! I'm so proud of you!"

Dad patted my head and smiled wide as he said, "I always knew you would accomplish great things. Becoming a goddess is totally a dramatic flair that fits you."

Kayden took me from Mom's arms and rested a hand against my cheek. "You scared ten years off my life."

Mason and Trey knelt on either side of me. Mason set his head against my shoulder and exhaled harshly. "I think twenty off of mine."

Trey smiled and patted my other shoulder. "You never cease to amaze me, my beautiful mate."

"Glad to keep you all on your toes," I teased.

Dhun whined and I pushed away my mates to hug him, being careful of his spines. "Thank you, friend. You helped win this war and ensure casualties were minimal."

He vibrated his spines and yipped happily. Once I released him, he walked over and sniffed at the silver lily that had grown and looked back at me.

Jol walked to it, knelt, and gently touched one petal. "You really were the prophesized one."

Mom and Dad knelt to examine the flower as well.

"It's full of magical power," Dad commented.

"You think it's safe to leave here?" Mom asked.

Dad tried to pull the flower from the ground and was thrown back by a powerful magical explosion.

I gasped and started to stand to go to him, but he hopped to his feet and shook his entire body, like a dog shaking off water. "Yeah, no one's going to be able to move that." His hair stood on end, looking like he'd been electrocuted.

Laughter bubbled out of me until I was on my hands and knees laughing so hard tears streamed down my face.

Nana Jolie, Great Aunt Leona, and all of their mates joined us, joining my laughter soon after hearing what happened to Dad.

Wiping my eyes, I turned to Mom and requested, "Mom, can you create a portal?"

"Where are you going?" Mason demanded and hovered at my shoulder as I stood, his hands moving erratically, like he was worried I was going to fall.

To be fair, I did wobble a little as I straightened, so the worry was not unfounded.

"The demons here need to return to their world and Jol and I need to go check on things," I explained. "With the Grand Advisor gone, we need to assess the world with fresh eyes. To see where things stand. Where the people stand. To see what's actually real."

"You need rest," Talrinir said as she approached us. "The females will assist King Jolmach in assessing the status of our world."

Azgon joined us, nodding. "You're not in any shape to face any further challenges. You have done more than enough today."

Mom created a portal to the castle. "Use the stone to communicate when you are ready to meet," she told Jol. "We will begin the steps to draft a peace treaty agreement so we can figure out a trade agreement and develop identification for your people to be able to visit here without issue."

Jol's eyes widened. "You will allow us to visit here?"

Nana Jolie and her mates had joined us at my back and Nana said, "Of course we will." I turned to look at her and she smiled softly as she added, "You are my granddaughter's people, after all."

My eyes welled with tears, and I threw my arms around her neck, sniffling loudly. "Nana."

She patted my back and whispered, "You did great today, Lily. You showed the world what you are capable of. Well done."

"I will be in touch," Jol said. I turned to face him and he bowed to me. "Goddess."

I would need to convince him to stop calling me that, but that wasn't a fight for today. "Your Majesty," I said and returned his bow. I started to stumble a step forward, but Trey wrapped his arm around my waist, holding me up so it hid my stumble.

Maya pushed her way through, my brother, Jaeden, and elf Tony on her heels. She hugged me tight and sniffled. "I was so scared you were going to explode."

Laughing, I patted her back and said, "Me, too."

"What?" Kayden shouted. "You thought you were going to explode, too?"

"For a second," I admitted. "There was so much power in me, like that time the shadows exploded out of me." The biggest worry had been for those nearest me.

Kayden growled. "Why do you insist on stressing us so much?"

"I think you just need to be more like Trey," I teased.

Trey looked down at me, his arm tightening a bit around my waist. "Like me?"

I nodded. "You're always so calm and collected."

He scoffed and shook his head. "I was just as freaked out as Kayden. I'm just not as vocal about it."

Kayden rolled his eyes. "He shouldn't get brownie points for having repressed emotions."

Mason snorted. "Yeah, we all know you'd win that battle."

"What?" Kayden shouted. "Who are you to talk about repressed emotions, bird brain?"

Laughter bubbled up and spilled out of me as my mates bickered with each other. Finally, it was over.

We had won.

The weakness I felt was disturbing, but my people were safe, so that was all that mattered.

"Shall we return home?" Trey asked. "You are in desperate need of a shower."

Looking down, I realized he was right. I was covered in dirt, blood, and debris.

Dhun yipped bye, and I raised my hand, watching him and the other demons go through the portal that Mom created.

Trey turned me away and we walked slowly towards our car.

Reporters shouted questions at us, but we ignored them, keeping our eyes focused on each other.

"I never would have thought there were multiple sirens," he whispered. "How did you realize it?"

"It just seemed insane to me that one person could be so much more powerful than Nana and Great Aunt Leona. To make us see different events at the same time is especially what convinced me there had to be more than one of them." It had been a guess, but it had paid off.

"I'm glad you're on our side," Kayden said. "That power was terrifying."

Taking a breath, I realized that I couldn't feel my shadow

serpent at all. "It may be gone," I admitted. "Something is gone."

Mason shook his head. "You used up a lot of magic. I'm sure once you're rested, you'll feel her again."

I hoped so.

"Can we have waffles?" I asked, my stomach grumbling hungrily.

"You can have whatever you want to eat," Trey said. "You did save all of our lives."

"What kind of mate would I be if I hadn't?" I teased and leaned my head against his shoulder.

Once home and showered, I lay on the couch staring up at the ceiling. The battle was over, we'd defeated the Grand Advisor and his assistant.

Yet, I knew this was really where things were going to get complicated.

"You're already stressing about tomorrow and you haven't finished today," Mason said as he knelt beside me. He pushed back some of my hair and kissed my cheek. "Live in the now."

Sighing, I said, "It's not that simple."

"Dinner!" Trey called.

Mason gripped my hands and pulled me to my feet. "For today, let it be that simple." His grip on my fingers tightened a moment and he whispered, "We almost lost you."

Throwing my arms around his neck, I buried my face in the crook and whispered, "I thought I'd lost you, too."

His arms encircled my waist, and he hugged me almost tight enough to bruise. "You're too reckless."

Scoffing, I whispered, "Pot meet kettle."

We both laughed and I felt us both settle a bit more.

He was right, I needed to relax tonight and tomorrow I could face the new battles.

After eating, we lay on the couch to watch comedy movies. Several had come out recently and with my head on Trey's thigh and my legs on Kayden's lap, I felt myself fully relax for the first time.

Mason sat in front of me and I ran my fingers through his hair. It was a bonding moment we definitely needed.

"Thank you," I whispered.

All three looked at me.

"For loving me. For being my mates. For trusting me during the battle."

"We're the ones who should thank you," Kayden said. "For giving us a second chance."

"Thank you for loving us," Mason said and kissed the inside of my wrist.

Trey's fingers traced down my jaw and he said, "Whether we deserve it or not, we are very thankful you accepted us."

I scoffed. "As if there was ever any doubt."

"Oh, there was," Kayden said and Mason nodded.

"However, just know that we love you and we will spend the rest of our lives showing you that," Trey said. He bent over and kissed my cheek. "I love you, Lily."

My heart felt like it was soaring. "I love you three, too."

CHAPTER
SIX

Warm hands slid up my thighs beneath the sheet covering me, waking me from sleep.

I stretched my arms up over my head and squealed as the stretch felt amazing. It seemed like I hadn't moved a muscle once I'd fallen asleep. Though, that was to be expected after using so much magic.

Kayden kissed my cheek before moving down and licking my neck. "Good morning, beautiful."

"Morning," I mumbled as I blinked my eyes open.

His hands inched higher, slowly, torturingly slowly.

Reaching down, I grabbed his hand and slid it beneath my underwear with a sigh.

He moaned and curled his fingers, sliding two inside of me as I arched up. "So wet," he moaned.

"No teasing, just pleasure today," I panted and turned to kiss him, our tongues twining together.

Pulling back, he smiled and said, "As you wish, Princess." Tossing the sheet back off the bed, he moved quickly to pull my underwear and shirt off. As my breasts met the cool air, my nipples immediately pebbled.

He groaned. "No bra?"

I shrugged. "Hadn't felt like putting one on last night."

"I'm definitely not complaining," he mumbled. Lowering down, he licked one nipple while rolling the other between his finger and thumb.

"What did I say?" I asked and pushed at his chest.

Smiling, he stood off the bed and pulled his boxers off, freeing his erection. "Apologies for keeping you waiting." Climbing back onto the bed, he settled over me and pressed the tip against my entrance that throbbed in anticipation.

When he didn't press inside, I wrapped my legs around him and thrust my hips up, burying him deep within me with a happy moan. "Yes!"

He kissed me on the lips, gripped my hips, and began to thrust into me, keeping my hips elevated.

I kissed and bit his neck and collarbone as he moved, his thrusts building the pressure until I screamed my release. My head fell back and I saw stars as our bond opened and his pleasure merged with my own.

"Oh, shit," Kayden muttered. "That's ... intense."

"More," I gasped and knocked his arm out from under him, flipped him onto his back, and rolled on top of him. I sank down immediately, seating myself on his hips with him fully buried inside of me. "Yes!" I screamed.

Mason walked in and his eyes widened when he saw me riding Kayden. "Want me to come back?" he asked.

I held out my hand. "No! Come here."

Kayden gripped my hips as I rode him, raising his hips to match my movements and add extra thrust.

Mason pulled his shirt off in one movement that was somehow really sexy, and the view of him shirtless, his muscles on display and his tattoos revealed was even sexier. He walked over to stand at the side of the bed, next to me. "What do you want?" he asked.

"Strip," I ordered, "then sit between his feet." Spinning around, I faced away from Kayden. He moaned and gripped my butt that was now facing him.

Mason kicked his pants and boxers off and sat between Kayden's feet, spreading his legs and stroked himself.

I leaned forward and took him into my mouth while I continued to ride Kayden.

Mason's hand slid into my hair, gripping it gently while I swirled my tongue around his erection. "Fuck," he whispered.

Mirroring my movements, I bobbed up and down on Mason's cock the same way I rode Kayden's.

It wasn't long before the three of our bonds opened and we all came in a sudden rush. The bonds were so new to us that controlling them sometimes was impossible. When it resulted in events like this, though, I wasn't complaining!

"Shower," Mason said as he picked me up and carried me to the bathroom.

After freshening up, we headed downstairs, where Trey had prepared breakfast.

Skipping through the kitchen, I wrapped my arms around his waist and pressed my cheek against his upper back. "Morning."

He turned around from the coffee he'd been making and hugged me, pressing a kiss to the top of my head. "Morning, gorgeous."

Tilting my head back, I asked, "What're our plans today?"

Pushing hair back from my face, his expression turned serious, worrying me. "You're still weak, so we're going to stay home and relax."

"Don't you need to go meet with the dragons?" Since he was a prince, he would usually need to go meet with the other royals to discuss the battle and what we needed to do for clean up or other remediation.

"No, there are enough dragons without me being there. You're more important than them anyway." He kissed my forehead and released me to push me towards the table. "Go sit and I'll bring your food."

"You really don't need to stay home because of me," I said, though I knew it would be in vain.

"You're incredibly weak," he said.

My glare earned me a smile in return. He wasn't wrong, but still ...

"It's important for you to rest and recuperate," Mason said as he pulled out a chair at the table for me. "The others can handle things for a couple of days."

"But –"

Kayden interrupted me. "We know you want to visit Jol, but you can't go out in public when you're not even capable of protecting yourself."

"Why do I need to protect myself when I have you

three?" I asked with a wide smile that earned me glares as expected. "Fine, I'll stay home today, but I want it known I object."

"Objection noted and dismissed," Trey said. He set a plate of bacon, sausage, eggs, toast, and sliced cherry tomatoes in front of me.

While they talked about a new videogame, I devoured every piece of food on the plate. It was delicious and I hadn't realized how hungry I was until I started eating.

"Still hungry?" Mason asked.

I shook my head, but he transferred a piece of buttered toast from his plate to mine and I immediately shoved it into my mouth. Okay, maybe I was still hungry.

Kayden stood and went to the pantry, grabbing something from inside.

"Do you want to play the new game we got?" Mason asked, distracting me. "It's multiplayer and Jolie said she thinks it's something you'll really enjoy."

Nana Jolie was really into videogames. In fact, before she'd met her mates, she'd been a writer for a videogame company. Now that she was queen, she had far less time to work on them, but I knew she still played a lot of games. She actually got Mom into videogames, too.

"If we're all going to play together, then that sounds fun," I agreed. If Nana thought I'd like it, that was good enough for me. She knew my taste as well as my mates.

"Only if it's not a romance game," Kayden said, as he returned and set a glass in front of me.

"What is this?" I asked as I sniffed at it.

"Protein shake," he explained. "You obviously need more nutrients and protein is important."

"What's wrong with romance games?" Trey asked with a smirk. "Is it because you're so bad at them?"

"I'm great with romance," he said, and at my scoff, he turned with wide eyes. "Did ... did you just scoff?"

"Uh, yeah. You are many things, Kayden, but romantic is not one of them."

His eyes narrowed. "Really? Then who is the most romantic of the three of us?"

"Mason," I answered immediately.

Trey choked on the bread he'd been eating. "What?" he demanded.

Mason smiled smugly and leaned back on the two back legs of his chair. "I may scowl a lot, but I'm not an idiot when it comes to my mate."

"What's something romantic he did?" Kayden asked.

"He took me shopping for a birthday present, even though he hates shopping, and he says things that are very romantic," I answered.

"Taking you out shopping isn't romantic," Trey countered and folded his arms over his chest.

"It is when it's something he despises, but he does it for me and doesn't grumble or look upset the entire time."

"I took you to the concert and got you a second shirt to wear," Kayden said.

"Yes, that was a great night," I said, and nodded.

"The real issue is we've been lacking in our romantic gestures in general," Trey said and let his arms fall. "I'm sorry."

"Kind of hard to do romantic gestures when I'm in another world you can't reach," I said with a soft laugh.

"We'll remedy that soon," he promised.

Someone knocked on the door, startling all of us.

"Who could it be?" I wondered and started to stand, but Mason gripped my arm, stilling me.

"I'll check," Trey said. Since it was technically his house and he was the highest ranked of my mates, I allowed it.

Plus, Kayden had put a piece of toast with jelly on my plate that had my attention.

"It's for you, Lily," Trey called.

I listened to two sets of footprints approaching and raised my eyes only for them to widen at the guest.

"Great Nana!" I gasped and leapt to my feet to run to her.

Great Nana Kara was one of the oldest elves, the mother of Great Uncle Silverowl and Grandpa Foxfire. She was also one of the most powerful healers in the world.

"Hello, Rubyserpent," she greeted. The elves were big on their animal-centered names and only elves received the extra name.

"What are you doing here?" I asked, concerned. She never showed up randomly, especially without her mate at her side.

"I brought her," Grandpa Foxfire said as he joined us, carrying several bags. "Boys, take these."

Mason and Kayden rushed over to take the bags from him.

"What's going on?" I asked, now suspicious, and took a step back from Great Nana.

She smiled and patted my cheek. "Smart girl. Be suspicious of even your family. However, you don't need to worry in this instance. I'm here to perform a check-up on you. Since you won't come to me and we all know you'd refuse your mother or Jolie, I'm here."

I opened my mouth and Trey swatted me on the butt. "Don't backtalk your great grandmother. The check-up will make us feel better as well."

Actually, I was fairly certain it would make them worry more.

"Come on, show me to the living room so we can do this check-up and set everyone's minds at ease. Your fathers, all of them, have been pestering me since the battle ended. I get a call from one just to hangup and have to answer a call from another one of them." She smiled warmly and said, "They're worried about their daughter and if they're worried, that makes me worried. You're one of my few great grandchildren, so let me ease my own worry."

With no other recourse, I took her arm and lead her to the living room. We both sat on the couch turned towards each other and she began using her magic to check me.

Her brows furrowed after the first second. "Lily, you're just like your mother and grandmother, you know that?"

"Because we don't like to worry people?" I asked with a wide smile.

She frowned at me. "Yes." She focused again before lowering her hands and sighing. "You've lost part of yourself; it's been burned out."

Frantically looking around, I was relieved to see my mates weren't in earshot. I leaned closer to her and whispered, "When I transformed into a goddess and channeled the demons' powers, it destroyed that power from every being able to be used again. My mates don't know, so please, keep it between us for now. I just need to go to the demon world for a recharge."

"It's more than that," she said gently and took my hand. "If you think returning there will help you recharge, then I will leave it at that for now. All I can do is provide you a bit of healing, since I can't fix the charred bits."

Charred? That was an interesting way to describe it.

She used her powers and shortly after starting, Grandpa Foxfire joined, using his powers as well for a bit more of a boost.

"What's the consensus?" Trey asked as he, Kayden, and Mason joined us in the living room.

"She's not one hundred percent better, but she's got some color back in her cheeks now." Great Nana patted one of my cheeks for emphasis. "And, she needs to go to the demon realm for a recharge soon."

"I'll let your dad know," Grandpa Foxfire said. "He's been communicating with King Jolmach and working on something with him."

"Thank you both for coming and checking on me," I said and hugged them each.

"Until your parents call you, stay inside and avoid public places, okay?" Grandpa Foxfire said, concern causing his brows to furrow. "Just in case."

"I know, even after saving the world there will be some who want to kill me."

"Being powerful is often more of a curse," Great Nana

said and patted my hand. "You're from a long family of females who suffer from it."

How true that statement was. My poor family.

CHAPTER
SEVEN

Maya threw down an ace of spades card atop the discard pile with a victorious smile. "I'm out! I win!"

Groaning, Piper and I threw the remaining cards in our hands down onto the discard pile in frustration.

"That's the third game in a row you've won! When did you get so good at this?" I asked enviously.

She collected the cards into a single pile, smiling and dancing a bit in her chair. "Jaeden's been playing with me and teaching me better techniques."

"Can he teach me?" Piper teased.

Narrowing her eyes, she sternly said, "No."

Laughing, I patted her hand. "Don't worry, Maya, neither Piper nor I want your future mate."

Her cheeks flushed. "We don't know he's going to be my mate yet."

I rolled my eyes.

Piper said, "Girl, he's an idiot if he doesn't choose you."

"We're taking things slowly and as they happen. I don't

want to rush things or do something to cause them to get scared," she whispered as she began shuffling the deck of cards.

"Only a mouse would be scared of you," Kayden teased as he entered the living room, carrying a tray with two wine glasses filled with bubbly liquid and two cherries each.

"Watch it, *fox*, or I'll burn your tail again," she threatened with a pleasant voice and smile.

The two of them had been like this ever since we were kids. In fact, she *had* burned his tail with her fire power and he'd cried for an hour even after it had healed, earning a scolding from Riddick.

"I think it's great that you're taking your time and courting them. However, I know you four will be great together." There was no doubt in my mind that they would end up her three mates. My brother had finally opened his eyes and seen that his childhood friend, and secret crush, liked him back and now he was all in.

Kayden set a drink down in front of Maya and I and kissed my cheek.

"Where's my drink?" Piper asked.

"You're working," he replied as he walked out of the room. "No drinking while you're guarding the princess."

She stuck her tongue out at his retreating back.

"They're still hovering, huh?" Maya asked softly, watching him go.

I nodded. "I'm still not one hundred percent recovered, so they're worried about me." Truthfully, I didn't know if I'd ever feel one hundred percent again now that I'd lost part of my power. Lost part of myself.

"Have you talked to King Jolmach recently?" Maya asked.

I nodded. "We spoke last night. Things are going well with the restoration, but slowly. It's hard to revitalize a world that's been kept burned and dead." Turned out, Valentino had been continuously burning and destroying the land to keep it in line with his lies to the demons.

There was a lot of work to be done still, though.

Mom and Dad still weren't letting me return to the demon world yet. They promised I could go soon, but for now, they were making me wait.

It was frustrating because I wanted to go back to see Talrinir and Azgon as well as the others. I kept thinking about the little demon orphan boy I'd met and wanting to return to help him as well as others as soon as possible.

"It's still terrifying to think about how powerful that man was. I'm glad you had an ace up your sleeve because watching you all fight was awful," Maya whispered and reached over to grip my hand.

"I'm her guard and I couldn't even get close to her. It was incredibly frustrating," Piper grumbled.

"Well, what's important is that we're all safe and sound and neither world was overthrown."

"What's important is that none of the royals died, especially you," Piper said and squeezed my shoulder. "You saved us and everyone is very, very thankful."

"So, what's your plan for the next few days?" Maya asked.

"No," I said immediately. "You're not hiding at my house to avoid the guys you are courting."

She pouted. "Mean."

Piper laughed loudly and Maya smacked her in the face with a pillow.

Piper gasped. "You did *not* just hit me in the face with a pillow."

"You laughed at me!" Maya countered, getting to her feet and backing around the couch as Piper grabbed a pillow and held it out menacingly.

Laughing, I watched as they chased each other around the couch, swinging pillows while also laughing.

Right, things didn't need to be perfect to enjoy them.

Relaxing was important for my recovery as well.

After Maya left and Piper went to her room to sleep, Trey joined me on the couch to watch a comedy. He draped his arm around my shoulders and pulled me against his side, absentmindedly rubbing his thumb along my arm.

"You seem a bit more relaxed," he commented.

I nodded. "It was nice having them here. They know just how to make me laugh."

"That sounds like a challenge," he muttered, but I didn't bother to comment.

Silly, jealous man.

"You're ridiculous," I muttered.

He smiled and squeezed my shoulders. "I know."

"So, what is up for tomorrow?" I asked.

"We are going to take you to work at the shop tomorrow," he commented. "You need to get some sleep. Am I keeping you up? Do I need to take you to bed?"

"Yes, take me to bed," I said immediately.

He snickered and gathered me into his arms to carry me up the stairs to my room. "As you wish, Princess."

I didn't respond because he was obviously being silly, but I loved being carried to my room by him. He climbed in, curled around me in the bed, and kept me warm throughout the night.

As I woke the next morning, he tightened his grip on me, purring as he nuzzled my neck. "Love."

I hugged him tighter. "Yes, all of the love."

"Mine."

"Yes, yours," I agreed."

"Good," he exhaled and relaxed.

That was ... unexpected. Why was he so relaxed by those statements?

"Forever," he whispered.

My heart thudded faster. "Yes, forever."

Was he still that worried about me that even in sleep he had to confirm I was still here and his?

Or was it just his possessive nature?

Gently, I stroked a hand up and down his back and his breathing quickly evened out.

Whatever the reason, I did enjoy waking up to warm hugs like this, so I let myself relax and sleep a bit more.

Mom kept her hand over my eyes as she made me walk towards something in the hybrid lands.

"Why can't I look where I'm going?" I asked as I almost tripped over a tree root for the third time.

"Because it's a surprise," she said with an exasperated sigh. "You've always been a pain about surprises."

"I just prefer to see where I'm going so I don't fall," I muttered. She was right, though. I hated surprises.

"Want me to carry you?" Kayden offered.

"No," I said immediately, making Mom laugh.

"It's about time you got here," Riddick said. "We could hear you trampling through the forest like an ogre for over a mile."

I growled at him, but that just made everyone laugh.

Everyone, I realized, included all of my fathers since there were four distinct male laughs.

Mom pulled her hand away, and I blinked at the bright sun, letting my eyes adjust.

At first, I wasn't sure what I was looking at, until Dhun hopped through and yipped at me.

A large, stone rectangle had been built upright, like a doorframe, including a door that was open on both sides, and within it swirled a portal. A portal to the demon world.

"How?" I breathed as I stepped forward.

Dhun pranced next to me, tongue hanging out the side of his mouth in joy.

"She had a little help," Grandpa Nico said as he tele-ported next to us.

"Honestly, it took them like two days to figure out how to make it stay open," Branson said.

"There was a lot of cursing," Triston agreed with a nod.

I hugged Mom and Grandpa Nico. "Thank you. Thank you."

"Anything for you," Mom whispered.

"I'm still waiting on that rainbow unicorn," I teased her.

She bumped my shoulder with hers while laughing. "Brat."

Turning back to the portal, I took a deep breath and said, "Really, though. Thank you for ... accepting this. Me. Everything."

"We always told you that we don't care what you become, that we will love you no matter what," Dad said and draped his arm around my shoulders. "Maybe now you'll believe us."

"So, this will always remain open?" I asked.

"There will be stipulations. The kings and queens all gathered to vote, and it was a unanimous decision to create portals for travel between worlds. We've signed the treaty with King Jolmach as well," Dad answered. "There will be other portals opened in the more public areas like the park as well, but this is the first one we were able to create. There will be guards at them all and guidelines for individuals crossing, too. An official announcement will go out in the next few days, now that we know we can create this."

"Well? What are you waiting for?" Mom asked. "I've got it on good authority there's a concerned demon king waiting on the other side."

Mason linked his hand with mine and said, "Well, we better not keep him waiting longer than necessary."

Trey and Kayden stepped up behind us, big smiles on their faces.

"Let's go see my people," I said. Looking at my parents, I added, "My *other* people."

Taking a deep breath, I stepped through the portal and was immediately hugged by Talrinir as she shouted, "Lily!"

We stood on a hill on the opposite side of the forest from the one that we'd first sent Dhun through, our first glimpse of the demon world. It was a fitting entrance view.

"Hello, friend," I greeted. "How are you?"

She released me and picked up a potted plant that was growing three, thick, green leaves. "We're ... thriving!"

I gently touched one of the leaves. "That's wonderful!"

Turning, my eyes widened as I took in the silver lily with red tipped flowers in the field on the far side of the forest. It was impressive that I could see it from so far, but was likely due to the magic it possessed. "How is the flower here?" I asked. "Isn't it in Jinla?"

"It's connected to both worlds since you are from both,"

Talrinir explained. "It shall live here forever, a reminder of the sacrifice you made."

"Sacrifice?" Trey asked.

I flinched, having not told them this yet. "I ... lost part of my powers in order to save everyone and use Goddess Mode."

"Why didn't you tell us?" Kayden asked, and set a hand on my arm. "Are you okay?"

I smiled and kissed his cheek. "It was worth it. I don't regret it."

Trey scowled. "Is that what Kara was scowling about when she came to treat you?"

Flinching, I nodded. "Yeah. Apparently, parts of my powers are ... charred."

Trey's eyes widened, and he reached out to grip one of my hands. "Charred?"

Smiling, I squeezed his hand. "I'm okay, Trey. In fact, since stepping foot in the demon world, I feel better than ever."

And I really did. In fact ...

Closing my eyes, I focused on my shifter powers and immediately, scales covered my body. "Oh, thank goodness."

"Lily," Mason growled, "were you unable to shift this whole time?"

Smiling as I opened my eyes, I laughed nervously. "Maybe."

Kayden squatted down with his head in his hands, groaning.

"Why didn't you tell us?" Trey demanded.

"Because I knew you'd react this way!" I snapped and shook my head. "I'm fine. Now, stop babying me."

Talrinir watched our interaction curiously and silently.

"Anyway, I'm fine. I feel great now."

Dhun pushed his head against the back of my legs, whining.

"Oh, he's in a rush," Talrinir said with a soft laugh. "King Jolmach has been waiting for you. He's got a surprise."

"Another surprise?" I whispered.

"Come," she turned and skipped down the hill, her dog-like ears flopping with each skip. "You're going to be so happy with how much we've already accomplished!"

"Apparently, Queen Jolie took your plans and started instituting them over the past few days," Trey whispered in my ear.

"My plans?"

He nodded. "You'll see."

I narrowed my eyes. How did he know things I didn't? Was he withholding anything else from me?

Following the excited Dhun, I gasped when we entered the castle's garden to find it full of green plants, blooming flowers, and trees. My hands flew to my mouth as tears built and my legs wobbled.

Jol and Great Uncle Silverowl turned at my gasp, both smiling when they saw me.

"Welcome back, Goddess," Jol greeted. "What do you think of our garden now?"

"How?" I asked.

Great Uncle Silverowl explained, "Several elves volunteered to come help with the demon world and they've found great success. It seems you started the healing of the land when you were here previously."

Right, the flowers I'd helped. I hadn't realized that that would also help now, though.

"We've got crops growing to help feed us for the next decade," Jol said proudly.

"They set up fields near the village," Azgon announced as she perched atop the garden wall.

Jol sighed. "Azgon, what have I told you about jumping over the wall?"

"Hello, Princess Lily," she greeted me, completely ignoring him and earning another sigh from the king.

"Hello, Princess Azgon," I greeted and curtsied.

She tittered and jumped down to come hug me. "Should I call you *Goddess* now as well?"

"No," I said and turned to Jol. "You've got to stop calling me that, too. I'm not a goddess."

"You literally turned into a goddess," he argued with a raised brow.

"Did you call Third to Reign, Goddess?" I asked and put my hands on my hips.

He scowled. "No."

"Well, then why would you call me that?"

"But ... you haven't reigned, so ..."

"If you wish to keep a title with my name, you may call me princess as that's the highest position I shall ever hold in either world."

He scowled, but Great Uncle Silverowl set his hand on Jol's shoulder and said, "You won't win this argument, friend. Best to accept what our precious Lily wants."

Jol exhaled and shook his head. "I don't think I've ever met a more stubborn female."

"No doubt," Kayden agreed.

I elbowed him in the stomach, knocking his breath from him.

Azgon squeezed my hand to get my attention again. "The females are asking for you to visit the village. Can you spare time?"

Jol waved me away as soon as I looked at him. "I still have business to discuss with Prince Silverowl. Go."

Azgon released my hand and leapt back up atop the wall. "Come on!"

Jol let out a long sigh. "Females," he mumbled.

Mason grabbed me around the waist and threw me up and over the wall. I managed to land on my feet without wobbling and jogged after Azgon, who had run off ahead.

Mason flew in his raven form beside me, his wings tinged slightly blue in the sunlight.

"Pretty bird," I crooned.

He made a strangled croak that I was fairly certain was a grunt of disapproval, which made me laugh as I continued running.

I could feel Kayden and Trey's amusement through our bond as well as they ran behind me.

Demons we passed bowed to me or made a symbol with their hands over their hearts.

I smiled at them all and as we ran across the open fields, I felt the freest I had in my entire life. I felt ... complete.

We arrived at the village and I greeted the females and children who I'd spent time with the last time I had been here. The children were much more welcoming, no longer scared of me, and huddled around with at least one of their hands clutching at my clothes or my arms and hands.

Druth hobbled out of her house and took my hands in hers, tears in her eyes. "Well done, Princess. You are a merit to the royal line. Third to Reign would be very proud of the woman you've become."

Tears built and I blinked them away. "Thank you, Druth."

"We requested your presence so you could tell us what happened," Druth explained. "So we can record it properly in our books. To ensure the truth will be recorded and never altered."

Following her, we headed to the logs around the fire and with my mates' help, we filled them in on the entire battle.

CHAPTER
NINE

We spent so long talking to Druth and the other females that we opted to spend the night in the village instead of traveling back to the portal and home.

Plus, I wanted to spend more time here.

Talrinir had a stone and let Jol know our decision. It piqued my interest that she was communicating directly with the lonely king. Perhaps he wasn't so lonely now?

Although they offered a bed, I chose instead to shift into my snake form and sleep beneath the stars, coiled up and relaxed. I chose a place near the fire, though I was warm enough without it. The moonlight made my scales shimmer and the billions of stars added to the light's reflection.

"You truly are magnificent," Trey praised as he lay on his side beside me, stroking a hand along my scales.

"And huge," Kayden said. He canted his head as he looked at my coiled state. "I think you grew since you returned home."

I hissed at him, which made all three of my mates smile.

"You appear more at ease here than in our world," Mason commented. "I can sense how relaxed you are, whereas at home you were on edge, even after the war was over and we were on the hybrid lands."

He didn't seem upset by it, more curious.

"Yes, that makes sense as she is the rightful heir to the throne, so the magic in this land recognizes her. Plus, all of us worship her as we did Third to Reign," Talrinir said as she joined us. "Actually, I believe she is worshipped more highly than Third to Reign now."

"We'd thought you had gone to bed," Kayden said.

She shrugged a shoulder and flipped one of her dog-like ears over her shoulder like I might my hair. "I couldn't sleep just yet."

"Why does it make sense that she feels more at ease here? She's a princess in our world as well, so why wouldn't she feel the same in both worlds?" Trey asked. A hint of jealousy seeped through our bond, startling me a bit.

"She's a princess in your world, but how many times have there been attempts on her life, attacks by those who either didn't like what she was or who her family was?"

All of my mates scowled, likely remembering the attack at my birthday party and the few others that had happened over the course of my life.

"Here, she was attacked a couple of times due to the Grand Advisor's trickery, but now … now she is a goddess. There are none who dislike her. She isn't ruling over us. She isn't making laws or rules we don't agree with. She did not save us for her personal gain. She rescued us because we are her people, because we were in need. She sacrificed a part of herself and left that reminder permanently glowing in the soil. She is safer here than your world and always will be. You, as her mates, and her descendants are as well."

She was right, I did feel safer here. It wasn't just the lack of attempts on my life, though. It was just the way the magic thrummed through the land. Yes, there was magic in our world, in Jinla, but it was so modernized that you could almost forget that magic existed. Well, at least until you saw a man turn into a dragon or teleport next to you. There were many magicless humans in the world who lived amongst us, but would never experience shifting or magic. Though, they were definitely the minority. With so many humans mating with shifters, I doubted it would be long before humans were almost extinct. Not that I wanted that, but it seemed likely based on what we had been seeing.

Here, everyone was a demon, no matter what powers or form they took. They didn't discriminate based on what kind of demon they were, they were just a demon. Unlike those in our world who hated hybrids so much that they had been hunting us. My father had died because of such hatred. Most demons here were equal, except for the Council and Jol. Would that change? Was he going to alter their structure now that the Grand Advisor was gone?

There would be a lot of changes to both worlds with ours now being connected, that was for certain. I hoped the changes were for the better of the world, though.

"The magic in the land recognizes her because of her blood?" Mason asked.

Talrinir nodded. "If she had fought the Grand Advisor

here, I think she would have defeated him quicker as the land would have given her however much magic she needed instead of her needing to use Jolmach as a conduit."

Crap, that would have been nice to know before. I would have pulled him into this world first.

"She even has a temple being built," Talrinir whispered as she looked up at the stars.

We all stared at her and I felt our combined disbelief through our bond.

"Temple?" Mason asked.

She nodded and dropped her chin to look at us again. "Some of the demons who had been part of the attack, who had seen her ordering your people not to kill them, are building it. Those who personally witnessed her goddess transformation and her mercy. There are currently multiple shrines built that people leave small gifts at. I've personally seen at least three shrines."

People were leaving gifts at shrines for me? That was ... insane! I was just a regular person. Sure, I had transformed, but I wasn't able to do that anymore.

"Her sacrifice, losing an ability, a part of herself, to save us, will never be forgotten by our people."

Hearing they had created shrines for me was somewhat uncomfortable. My family had saved their people many times without such thanks. What I had done wasn't that special.

"There is also a residence being constructed," Talrinir continued.

"A residence?" Trey asked.

She nodded, and her ears flapped a bit in her excitement. "For you and any children you may have."

Kayden looked at me. "Did you decide to live here without telling us?"

Talrinir responded in my stead. "We have been constructing it without her knowledge. This is the first she has heard of it as well. While we would love for you to live here permanently, this residence is also for when you are visiting. I'm sure King Jolmach has no issue providing you a room, but we wanted you to have your own space. It is up to you to determine how often you stay."

Living here did sound nice. I could be here to continue helping them rebuild and help with the orphans, something I planned to discuss with Jol tomorrow. Plus, with the portals, I could visit my family whenever we wanted to.

But ... I had to also take into account Kayden, Mason, and Trey's desires.

Trey was a prince after all, even if it was unlikely that he would end up ruling.

And living here would mean losing some of our comforts, like videogames. At least until we figured out a way to get them electricity.

"Thank you for letting us know. We will have to discuss it," Trey said with a polite smile.

She stood, stretched, and smiled. "Great! Well, I'm going to try to sleep. See you tomorrow."

"It is really peaceful here," Mason commented and set a hand on me. "I can understand why Lily feels so content."

"Talrinir is right, it's late and we should sleep. We can discuss it tomorrow." Trey stepped away, shifted into his dragon form, and curled up. I also felt him put up a wall through the bond, keeping us from knowing what he was feeling.

"Grumpy," Kayden muttered before following suit.

Was he grumpy, or was it something else?

CHAPTER
TEN

There were several heavy objects on me, wrapped around and between my coils.

Opening my eyes, I was shocked to find four kids between the ages of two and four as those objects.

"You were having a nightmare and suddenly these kids rushed from the houses or places they were sleeping over to you. As soon as they lay with you, you settled," Talrinir explained with a soft smile.

The kids raised their heads, blinking sleepily, and I recognized one of them as the orphan boy I'd spoken to in the demon city when I'd gone exploring. His name was ... Elrith? Yes, Elrith! He had small, thick horns at the top of his head and a tail wrapped around his waist like a belt as he sat with an arm around one of my coils. His skin was covered in scales, similar to that of a dragon, though I noticed they seemed to be a different color and thickness now than the first time I had seen him. They looked stonelike. Was it because he was growing? Had he shed the previous scales to grow the new ones, or did they just change?

Shifting into my human form, I helped the kids brush off the dust and the little boy smiled at me.

"You're the hornless lady!" he said excitedly. "I thought you smelled familiar."

"Her name is Princess Liliana," Talrinir explained.

He gasped. "The one who saved us? Who saved the demons? That was her?"

Talrinir nodded. "That was her."

I nodded as well and said, "It's nice to see you again, Elrith."

His eyes widened, his tail wagged back and forth wildly, and he smiled wide, showing off his thick, vampire-like twin fangs. "You remembered my name!"

"Of course I remember your name, Elrith. Do you live here now?"

He shook his head and said, "I don't live here. I was passing by and saw the fire, so I came to investigate, then fell asleep at the fire."

"Have you eaten recently?" I asked as my own stomach grumbled.

His stomach grumbled in reply and he rested a hand on it. "Not for two days."

Talrinir growled softly, most likely upset to find this out. She looked at me and said, "King Jolmach has requested you meet him at the castle for breakfast. Would you like me to tell him you'll be bringing a friend?"

I smirked and said, "You two seem much closer. Do you have something to talk to me about?"

She flushed and turned her head. "Later, nosey princess. I'll just tell him you're bringing Elrith."

Chuckling, I stood and stretched, squealing as I did.

The little boy laughed. "You have funny skin and make funny noises."

"Would you like to come have breakfast with me?" I asked him and held out my hand.

He looked at it nervously for a moment, looked up into my eyes, and asked, "Will you protect me, Princess?"

The fact that he had to ask made me simultaneously angry and sad and my hair began to glow from the emotions. Squatting down so we were eye level, I nodded and set my hand on his shoulder. "While you are with me, my mates and I will keep you safe. Promise." I made an x over my heart with my finger and smiled warmly at him, understanding the uncertainty he felt.

He reached out and touched a piece of my glowing hair. His expression changed to a look of deep contemplation, or as much as a child could hold that expression, and he nodded. "Okay, Princess. I'll join you for breakfast." I wasn't sure what he'd considered while looking at my hair, but I was glad for the result.

Trey squatted down next to me and Elrith focused on him nervously. "I see you have scales; they're similar to mine."

Elrith's brows furrowed in confusion as he looked at Trey's smooth, human skin, but Trey let his dragon scales flow over and then Elrith's brows rose in delight. "Wow! You can shift your skin like the princess!"

"Are you able to shift?" Trey asked him. "Into an animal or other form?"

Elrith looked at Talrinir nervously before looking down at the ground and clenched his hands in front of him without answering.

Why would he be nervous about telling Talrinir he could shift? They had demons who shifted, didn't they? "We should start our journey so we aren't late and we can talk on the way?" I suggested.

"Visit us again soon!" Druth called out from the front of her house.

I raised my hand and smiled. "I will." Walking to Talrinir, I pulled her into a hug and whispered into her ear, "I'll be in touch soon since we have *so much* to talk about."

She hugged me back, then pushed me away gently. "Anyone ever tell you that you are a brat?"

"All the time," Kayden said as he draped his arm around my shoulders and pressed a kiss to my cheek. "One of the biggest brats in both the worlds."

I pinched his side and skipped over to Elrith, holding my hand out for him to take. "Come on, Elrith. Let's head for the castle. I'm hungry!"

He set his hand in mine and after watching me skip a moment, started skipping as well, giggling with a huge smile on his face. "What is this?"

"It's called skipping," Kayden answered as he skipped by us, swinging his arms exaggeratedly.

"It's fun!" Elrith exclaimed, and let go of my hand to skip faster after Kayden.

Once we were far enough from the village that no one

could see us, Kayden shifted into his werewolf warrior form before continuing to skip.

Elrith slid to a stop. "Y-Y-You shift?"

"We can all shift," I explained gently and shifted into my warrior form.

Mason shifted into his bird form and flew overhead. "Hybrids," he cawed.

Trey shifted into his full dragon form for a moment, letting Elrith gawk.

"Can you shift, too?" I asked softly.

Elrith looked at me and my mates and asked, "Promise not to tell others?"

Although I wanted to ask why he didn't want others to know, I nodded and saved the question for later. "Promise."

Taking a breath, he closed his eyes, and we all stared in disbelief as his body rippled, black smoke exploded out of him, covering him and hiding him from our sight briefly. When the smoke dissipated, a three foot tall Elrith with the same horns, scale-covered skin, and fangs stood, but he now had red eyes, wings that looked to be made of the same stonelike substance as the scales on his skin, and claws growing from his fingers.

"He looks like a gargoyle," Mason whispered in my ear.

I nodded my agreement and quickly schooled my features so I was smiling as I approached Elrith. The last thing I wanted was for him to assume we thought him strange. I knew from experience how that felt. "You look awesome!" I praised. "May I touch your wings?"

He nodded.

Stroking a finger down the top of one of his wings, my eyes widened to realize they felt like stone as well.

"Father said I wasn't supposed to show others because even though demons are different, I'm very different. *Too* different," he explained in a whisper.

My chest hurt, feeling that familiar pang. "I understand being different," I told him. "However, I think you look amazing."

"Do you have abilities?" Trey asked him.

"Abilities?" Elrith asked back.

"Like breathing fire," Trey explained as he stood before him.

Elrith shrugged. "I don't know. I'm not supposed to be in this form much, unless my life is in danger."

I'd thought it before, but he was incredibly articulate for being so young. Was it due to being alone and needing to survive? Or had someone been teaching him? More questions for later.

"You can shift back," I told him. "Thank you for trusting us and showing us."

The black smoke swirled around him and then dissipated to reveal him back in his demon form. "Are you going to tell others?" he asked. "Are you going to tell the king?"

"I think King Jolmach would think you are awesome, just like I do, but if you don't want me to tell him, I won't." I gripped his little hand in mine and said, "I promised to protect you, remember? Me and my mates. Right, guys?"

All three of my mates nodded.

Elrith smiled at me and said, "I'm glad you're here,

Princess. You make me feel safe. It's been ... I haven't felt safe much."

My hand shot to my chest as it hurt and I pulled Elrith into a tight hug. "I'm glad you feel safe with us."

"Come on, we better hurry or King Jolmach will eat all the breakfast," Kayden teased. "Elrith, want to race?"

"Race?" he asked as I reluctantly released him. The urge to cuddle him against my chest and protect him from the world roared through my veins.

Kayden nodded. "I'll race you to the castle. Loser has to give the winner his bread roll."

Elrith gasped and took off at a sprint towards the castle.

Mason and I laughed as Kayden ran after him.

"Is this feeling what I think it is?" Trey asked me as he and Mason jogged on either side of me. We moved just fast enough to keep Kayden and Elrith in our sight, but not fast enough to pass them.

"What?" I asked, confused.

"Did we just adopt our first child?" he clarified with a soft smile and reached over, squeezing my hand.

"You're okay with it?" I asked, shocked by the happy feeling flowing through our bond. I had planned to talk to them about it once we all had a moment alone.

"If we weren't together, I would have adopted him if you hadn't," Trey answered.

"Same," Mason replied with a nod.

My heart warmed at their replies. I was so lucky to have them as mates.

I smiled up at my handsome dragon prince and asked,

"Do you think my parents will be shocked when we come home and introduce them to their first grandchild?"

Trey laughed. "No, they'll fawn over him just like Dan did you."

Mason nodded in agreement. "Dan will probably steal him like he stole you all the time."

"Jolie is going to turn into mush the first she sees him," Trey said with a soft smile.

I nodded. "Nana Jolie is definitely going to be excited."

My adoptive family was seriously the best. I hoped Elrith would feel the same as he grew older. But first, we had to convince him to *let* us adopt him.

Elrith danced in a circle, his tail swishing in his excitement. "I won! I won! I get your bread roll."

Kayden panted in an overexaggerated manner at the doorway to the castle. "Yes, you won. You're very fast."

"Have to be," Elrith said. "The faster the safer."

He wasn't wrong, but it made me angry to hear him say it, to know that he endured so much alone. My hair once again started glowing, casting rainbows around us.

Mason slid his hand into mine and squeezed. "Deep breath, babe."

Closing my eyes, one deep breath turned into two before I finally felt the anger disappear.

"Little goddess," Jol called as he exited the castle doors, a smile on his face.

Mason released my hand so I could step forward and hug Jol. "Hello, Jol. How are you today?"

He patted my back, set his hands on my shoulders, and smiled down at me. "I'm much better now that you're here."

"No," Mason said and pulled me back against him with an arm around my waist. "No more men for you."

Jol and I shared a smile before he looked over at Elrith who was slightly hiding behind Kayden. "And who is this?"

"Elrith, come here, please," I called gently and held out my hand.

He hesitated a moment before Kayden stepped forward, giving him a way to stay hidden and make his way to me. Once he took my hand, his nerves settled a bit and he straightened to look at Jol.

"King Jolmach, this is Elrith. Elrith, this is King Jolmach. We are friends, so you don't need to fear him," I explained.

Jol squatted down and smiled at Elrith. "Hello, imp. Your horns are thick for your size. How old are you?"

"I'm five, King," he answered, meeting Jol's eyes, a bit of pride shining in his eyes at the compliment from Jol about his horns.

"Well, when I heard a guest was coming with our goddess, I had them make an extra special breakfast including things from the other world. Would you like to join us?"

Elrith nodded enthusiastically. "I've not eaten for two days as I missed the meals at the city."

Jol scowled. "You missed them?"

Elrith nodded again. "I was trying to hunt in the woods and when I didn't find anything, I went to the city, but they were already closed."

"Ah, I see. Let's not delay then, and head in so we can eat. I don't want my people going hungry," Jol said and stood.

I squeezed Elrith's hand and smiled down at him as we

followed behind Jol. He returned my smile and I knew my heart was already his. This little boy was never going to go hungry again.

"Did your discussions with Silverowl go well?" I asked Jol as we followed him down the hallway, and out to the garden where a large table was set up and filled with food.

"Yes, though we still have more to work out. There are meetings tonight with your kings and queens. Will you be in attendance?" He pulled out a chair for me and I sat in it with a smile of thanks.

"I wasn't informed about it, so they must not think I need to be there," I answered.

"I would like you to attend, if you have the time," he said as he pushed in my chair and then pulled out the chair beside me for Elrith who hopped up into it, mouth open and practically drooling at the sight of all of the food on the table.

"We do not have plans tonight," Trey said before I could even ask. "You are available to attend if you wish."

I nodded. "Then we will attend."

Jol sat and smiled. "Wonderful. That makes me feel better. Please, eat."

Elrith sat perfectly still and I could tell he was uncertain what he was allowed to do.

Mason sat on his other side, so he picked up Elrith's plate and asked, "Are there any foods you see that you don't want to eat?"

Elrith frowned and shook his head. "I eat all edidble."

"Edible," I whispered to correct him.

"Edible," he corrected.

Mason piled Elrith's plate high with food and set it before him. "If you finish this and want more, you just let me know, okay?"

Elrith's eyes welled a moment and he nodded. "Okay."

Kayden grabbed a bread roll and set it on Elrith's plate, giving him two now. "For winning our race."

Elrith smiled and popped the entire roll into his mouth, chewing with unadulterated delight.

Jol took my plate before any of my mates could and filled it up, then set it in front of me. "How are you feeling now that it's been a bit since the battle?"

"Still a little drained," I admitted, which caused all three of my mates' heads to whip in my direction. "Losing that piece has definitely caused a change in me that I think I'm just not used to yet."

"Have you been able to summon your serpent?" he asked.

"She was a snake this morning," Elrith commented.

"He meant my shadow snake," I explained to Elrith, whose eyes widened.

"You have a shadow, too?"

Jol paused with his fork midway to his mouth and raised his eyes to look at Elrith.

"I think our shadows are slightly different," I explained. "Can yours form into a shape?"

Elrith frowned. "Not a creature shape, but it can be a ball. To protect."

"Interesting," I said and smiled warmly at him. "We'll have to do some training later."

Elrith gasped and gripped my forearm. "Really? You'll train me?"

"Yes," I said and nodded.

He jumped up in his seat and did a little dance. "Yay!"

Kayden and Mason snickered into their hands and turned their heads so he wouldn't see their laughter.

"Sit and eat," I ordered, though not sternly. "You need to fill your belly so you can stay strong."

"Yes, Princess," he said, plopped down, and began shoveling bites of food into his mouth.

We ate the rest of the meal in silence and once Jol and I were done, we walked to the far corner of the garden.

"I'd like your approval to help create an orphanage here," I told him. "For those like Elrith."

"You may build whatever you see fit. I will have Zoman assist you. Just tell him what you need and he will ensure it happens."

"Thank you. I appreciate that. I want to do as much as I can for the children here. Creating an orphanage where they can sleep feeling safe is the least I can do."

"Will you put Elrith in the orphanage?" he asked as he examined the leaf of a small plant at his feet.

"That will be up to Elrith, but my mates and I plan to offer to adopt him," I answered.

He smiled as he raised his head and said, "I figured as much."

"Do you have many demons with the ability to shift?" I asked. "Or use shadows?"

He straightened and frowned. "Shifting is not an ability of our kind. We are as we are. The shadows are a different story. In my lifetime, I have only known a handful who could use the shadows, and those were all very powerful demons, such as Third to Reign and you."

Could Elrith be a hybrid? Was it possible that his parents weren't full demon and that's why he could shift?

"Is this regarding the boy?" he asked.

"I can't say as I've made a promise, but I'll do some investigating and update you when I can," I answered.

He smiled warmly and said, "I understand and will not pressure you to answer. I hope you know that I do not discriminate, though, on what powers or not my people possess."

I nodded. "I know, but it seems some are uncertain."

"Are you truly okay?" he asked, his smile falling. "You seem ... drawn."

"When I used that power to become a goddess, to take down the Grand Advisor, it felt like a piece of me was burned away. Destroyed. It was more than an overuse of my powers. It was like I cut off a piece of myself and cauterized it. I knew when I used the power I would have to sacrifice a part of myself and I would do it again without hesitation. It's just taking me a little longer than I anticipated to feel like myself again."

He set his hand on my shoulder and squeezed. "If there is anything I can do, you let me know and I will do it immediately. This world, including me, owe you a debt we could never repay. Even if you asked for the throne, I would gladly hand it over."

I set my hand atop his on my shoulder and smiled. "The prophecy said I would give you the throne, remember? Plus, you've done so much for our people and I know deep down that you are the rightful ruler." It was like a bone deep knowledge. "Though, I do hope you continue taking my advice on matters."

He squeezed my shoulder and said, "Always."

CHAPTER
TWELVE

Dhun raced into the garden, his spines rattling as he slid to a stop before me. He yipped loudly and pranced around me in a circle.

"Dhun!" I gasped and dropped to my knees to hug him. "You're so big now!" He was even larger than when I'd seen him at the battle. "Are you ever going to stop growing?"

"He's the largest hellhound we have record of," Jol commented. "Druth couldn't believe her eyes when she saw him."

Elrith ran over and stood between Dhun and I. "Get back!" he shouted and growled. He pushed me with his tail, trying to get me to back up.

Dhun's ears lowered, and he backed up a step, whining.

"It's okay, Elrith. Dhun is my friend."

"Hellhounds aren't friends!" he growled. Black smoke began to seep from his feet and swirl up his legs.

"Elrith," I whispered and set a hand on his back, "you can't judge all hellhounds based on a few bad ones."

"They're evil," he growled. His tail lashed back and forth behind him, and I could feel him shaking beneath my hand.

I wasn't certain what trauma he'd faced from hellhounds, but it was clearly bad.

Jol squatted down beside Dhun and set a hand on him while keeping eye contact with Elrith. "I understand your desire to protect Princess Lily, but Dhun is not her enemy. Dhun and she are friends. Dhun protected her during the battle."

"He saved us," I agreed with a nod.

Elrith's eyes darted up to mine before he focused back on Dhun. "S-Saved you, Princess?"

"Yes," I replied. "Saved us all. Without Dhun's help, we might not have defeated the Grand Advisor or saved our worlds. I would have died."

The black smoke disappeared and Elrith took a step back so he was beside me instead of in front of me. "I see."

Dhun canted his head and whined.

"Elrith, can you help me water these plants?" Jol requested as he stood and moved towards a set of planter boxes.

"You okay here?" Elrith asked me.

I smiled and nodded. "Go help King Jolmach. I'll be fine."

He gave one last look at Dhun before jogging after Jol.

"Don't be too upset with him," I whispered to Dhun. "He's had a rough time."

Dhun huffed and sat before me.

I stroked between his ears and laughed softly. "Thanks for being understanding, friend."

"We should head back soon," Trey said as he stood beside me. "I need to meet with my father."

"Right." I stood and walked over to Elrith, who was sprinkling water from a watering can onto a pot with strawberry plants. "Elrith, I have a proposition for you."

He set the can down and tilted his head up to look at me. "Prop-i-shun?"

"A proposition is an offer," I explained. "You told me when I met you that your parents are dead now and that you're living on your own."

He nodded. "Yes."

"My mates and I don't like that idea. You see, we're fond of you and we would like to offer to adopt you. Would you like to come live with us? You'll always have food, a comfortable place to sleep, and we will protect you. You would become part of our family. How does that sound?"

His eyes widened. "You become my family?"

I squatted down so we could be eye level and nodded. "Yes. We would be your new family."

"What price?" he asked and took an uncertain step back.

"No price," I said, understanding his hesitation. "I was an orphan like you once, too. I was adopted and I want to give you that opportunity as well. You don't have to accept, though I want you to. We are going to open an orphanage here, a place for all of the other kids without parents. If you don't want to live with us, you could live with the other orphans in the orphanage instead. It's up to you, and we will respect whatever choice you make."

He looked at Jol who stood nearby watering other plants. "King?"

Jol set his can down and faced Elrith. "Yes?" I loved that he gave him his full attention, not belittling him or treating him differently. That was part of why I knew Jol was the perfect king.

"Is it okay to be adopted by Princess?" Elrith asked softly.

Jol smiled. "It is a great honor to be offered to be adopted by the princess, to become her son. I would accept if I were you."

Elrith turned with wide eyes. "I would be your son? I accept!"

I pulled him into a hug and he giggled as I rubbed my face against his. "I'm so happy!" Warmth spread throughout my body and I felt true joy at his acceptance.

"Also, since you agreed, you will become prince," Jol added as I released Elrith.

His eyes widened. "I agree again!"

We all laughed, including Dhun.

I held out my hand. "Come on, Prince Elrith. Let me take you to my world and introduce you to my family."

He took my hand and looked at Trey, Mason, and Kayden, who stood near the exit. "Does that mean they're my new fathers?"

I nodded. "Yes."

"You teach me to fight so I can help protect new mom?" he asked.

My eyes widened. He wanted to learn to fight to protect me? Not himself?

Understanding hit me in the gut, making tears well in my eyes. If he lost his parents to a hellhound, had to watch his mother die, perhaps that was why he didn't like Dhun and why he wanted to protect me.

All three of my mates nodded in answer to his question.

"Yes, we will train you to be the strongest you can be," Trey answered. "To protect yourself and those you love."

"Yay!" he shouted.

"I'll see you tonight, right?" Jol asked as he walked with us out of the garden.

"Yes, we'll return with my parents for the meeting," I agreed.

"Elrith, do you have any belongings?" Mason asked. "Anything you want us to get before we leave?"

Elrith nodded. "One bag."

"Can you lead us to it?" Mason requested.

"Okay," he agreed. He looked up at me and asked, "Can you fly?"

Was his bag up high somewhere? "No, I don't have the ability to fly, but Trey and Mason can fly, and I can ride Trey."

Elrith nodded and started running, pulling me along behind him. "Not too far," he called over his shoulder.

We ran away from the castle, towards the mountains. At the base of the mountains, Elrith looked all around before he shifted and used his wings to fly up into the air.

Mason shifted into his raven form and followed after him.

Trey shifted and bent down so Kayden and I could climb on his back.

"I can't remember the last time I rode a dragon," I commented.

"*It was just two nights ago,*" Trey said mentally through our bond.

My head fell back as I laughed. "I didn't mean *that* kind of riding. Dirty dragon."

Elrith led us to a small outcropping on the mountain that was barely big enough for Trey to land as a dragon, so he immediately shifted after landing.

Elrith climbed inside of a tiny hole, barely large enough for me to fit, and climbed back out with a small bag in front of him. "Okay. Ready."

"You sure there's nothing else?" Kayden asked.

Elrith nodded. "Just this."

We were all staring at the bag, curiosity circulating through our bond. What was in the bag?

"Alright!" I said with a wide smile. "Let's head to the portal."

"You sure I can go through?" Elrith asked and fidgeted with the bag in his hands.

"I'm Princess of both worlds, remember? And as my son, you are welcome in both worlds as well. Just be sure you only go through the portal with one of us, or my family, okay?"

He nodded. "'kay."

THIRTEEN

As soon as we stepped through the portal, Dad teleported to us.

His scowl turned into a smile when he saw us. "Welcome home!" He pulled me into a hug and I returned it, squeezing him tight.

"Thanks, Dad."

"Did you think we were unauthorized demons entering?" Trey asked.

Dad nodded. "We left it open so you could come home, but we had a couple more animalistic demons come through that we had to send back. After discussing with Jol, we decided that we would need to lock the portal except for authorized entries until we finalize how we're going to handle things. A topic for tonight's meeting."

"We'll be attending the meeting as well, at Jol's request," I explained.

He nodded, then drew in a deep breath and pushed me gently to the side to look behind me. "Who is this?"

Elrith hid behind Mason, the top of his head and his eyes peeking out from behind Mason's leg.

I held out my hand and Elrith walked forward to take it, his tail wrapped around his waist, something I was beginning to understand was a sign of unease.

I picked him up and held him on my hip so he was higher and felt him relax a little with my arm around him. "Elrith, I would like you to meet my adoptive father. This is Caleb, King of the Hybrids."

"King?" Elrith asked in a whisper.

I nodded. Looking at Dad, I said, "Dad, meet your grandson, Elrith."

Dad's eyes widened a second before immediately sparkling. A huge smile split his face. "Hello, cub. I'm excited to meet you!" He held out his hand and Elrith shook it.

"You want to know something fun?" I asked Elrith.

He nodded.

"Your new grandfather here can shift into *lots* of forms."

"He shifts, too?" Elrith gasped.

Dad's eyes widened as he looked from Elrith to me.

"Dad, can you show him your dragon form?" I requested.

He immediately shifted into his full dragon form and Elrith squealed in delight. "Scales! Like me!"

"Elrith, can you show Grandpa Caleb your form?" I requested.

He hesitated, but nodded. "Okay, Mama."

A zing of such powerful joy shot through me that I nearly dropped him as I was setting him down at hearing him call me that. I'd thought it would take him a while to refer to me that way, so it was unexpected to hear it so soon. Perhaps being alone for so long had made him desperate for a family again. Being so young, I could understand.

Once on his feet, Elrith took a breath and the smoke curled around him as he shifted.

Dad shifted from his dragon form to his human form and knelt in front of Elrith, examining him. "You are amazing," he praised. "Your scales are harder than mine!" He poked a fingernail against one of the scales, smiling wide.

Elrith beamed with pride.

"Why don't we go meet your other grandfathers and grandmother?" I suggested. "I'm sure they've got some yummy snacks inside."

Elrith squealed. "Snacks!"

I picked him up and swung him around onto my back, giving him a piggyback ride. "Let's go get snacks!" Jogging slowly, holding onto his arms around my neck, I made sure he didn't fall as we went.

Elrith laughed loudly, and I knew we were both smiling like fools as we approached the house.

Dad and my mates whispered behind us, but I dismissed them, since they were likely filling him in on what had happened.

Mom opened the door as I approached. "My baby's home!" She ran out to tackle me, but stopped when she saw Elrith. "Oh, an adorable visitor!"

"Mom, this is your grandson, Elrith. Elrith, this is Queen Ember of the Hybrids."

"Does she shift, too?" Elrith asked.

I nodded. "All hybrids shift. Grandma here can even shift into a bunny!"

"A bunny? What's a bunny?" he asked.

Setting him on his feet, he tilted his head slightly, confused.

"It's a prey animal," I explained. "Small, furry, and cute."

"Also delicious in stew," Dad teased as he caught up and kissed Mom on the cheek.

Mom shifted into her bunny form and then into her hybrid form, which was mostly humanoid with her legs rabbit-like to allow her to jump higher and a puffy white rabbit tail on her butt. "I prefer this form since I'm bigger." She winked.

Elrith giggled. "You're all so funny!"

"Mom, are there snacks?" I asked.

She gasped. "Of course! Come on, Grandson. I'll show you where I keep the good snacks." She leaned close to him and whispered, "The ones I have to hide from Grandpa Caleb."

"What? What snacks do you hide from me?" Dad gasped in not so fake shock.

Elrith laughed and took Mom's hand, letting her lead him inside.

"How many words out of his mouth before Nana Jolie melts into a puddle?" I asked Dad as we watched them go inside.

"Zero," he said. "She'll melt as soon as she sees him." He put his arm around my shoulders and squeezed. "He reminds me of you. Small, smart, and full of magic."

"I think he's a hybrid," I whispered. "He can do things the other demons can't, like shift."

"Well, we've got the first hybrid demoness right here," Dad said, squeezing me again. "So, it's not out of the realm of possibility. He did smell like a hybrid, but I will need to smell him again to tell what kind." He looked down at me and asked, "Are you feeling well?"

I shrugged. "As well as I can in the circumstances."

"You should visit Nana Kara for some healing," he suggested.

"Great Nana Kara already visited me. I think it's just going to take time to get used to not having that part of me. I'll be fine." I hugged him and said, "Thank you for worrying about me, though."

"Always, Daughter."

"Where's my granddaughter?" Nana Jolie shouted suddenly behind us.

We both spun around, staring at Nana Jolie and Grandpa Nico who must have teleported here.

"What are you two doing here?" Dad asked.

Nana Jolie shoved Dad to the side and pulled me into a hug. "There you are! You naughty little thing. You haven't visited me since the battle and I've been worried."

Laughing, I hugged her back. "Sorry, Nana."

"She has news for you," Dad said.

Nana pushed me back. "What?"

"I've brought you a great grandson," I explained.

Her mouth dropped open and she pushed by me, running into the house.

"Once there's a younger generation, you get shoved to the side," Dad said with a sigh and draped an arm around my shoulders. "Welcome to the club."

We all laughed, but our laughter doubled when we heard her delighted squeal when she saw Elrith.

CHAPTER
FOURTEEN

"I agree that we need guards stationed at the portals," I said as we sat in the meeting with all the kings and queens and Jol. "Due to the portals being a space to simply walk through, you are more likely to have animals crossing if it's not guarded, which could lead to a lot of unexpected issues if the animals begin crossbreeding."

"Exactly," Great Uncle Silverowl said with a nod. "My main concern isn't the people crossing, but the potential devastation of our flora and fauna."

"Where are we at with the identification for the demons?" Dad asked.

"We're going to give the demons two of our cameras and card printers. Since demons don't have different races among them, we will simply put demon as their ethnicity and since most can't shift, we will only need to put one picture," Mom said.

In this world, we had two pictures on our cards, one of us in human form and one in shifted form to make it easier for us to be identified. It was something people complained about for us hybrids who had multiple forms, like Dad, since he had so many different forms he could take, but was only identified with one. It *did* say hybrid on his card, though.

After several other discussions, the meeting ended and I was able to go around the table to where Grandpa Rhys sat. The Dragon King was slumped in his chair, but his aura was still imposing. I wasn't sure why, but he had scared me the longest, even though the dragon form was one of Dad's favorites.

At my approach, he looked up and smiled, his blue eyes sparkling with warmth. "Hello, Lily." Even as imposing as he was, Grandpa had always been incredibly sweet and spoiled me almost as much as Nana Jolie. He had helped me a lot with learning how to make my scales appear on certain parts of my body, something that was great for protecting vital organs in a battle.

"Grandpa Rhys, I'm going to build an orphanage in the demon world. Can you provide me a copy of the blueprints from the orphanage I built here?" I requested.

His smile widened as he nodded. "Of course." Almost immediately, his smile wilted a bit and he said, "We should discuss building materials, though. The demon world does not have the same materials available to them."

"We have rocks and brick," Jol said, overhearing our conversation since he was seated just two chairs over.

"I plan to transport concrete in bags and take a few mixers to utilize," I explained.

"Give me a day to think about it and I'll come up with a solution," Grandpa Rhys said. "I may have some other alternatives that will make building it even easier, but keep it safe and secure for the children."

"Thank you."

He smiled. "Anything for the savior of the two worlds."

I shook my head. "You guys have saved Jinla and the world before, so don't start that with me."

"Are you going to put a barrier around the orphanage?" Grandpa Nico asked and pushed off from the wall where he'd been leaning.

I nodded. "Once it's built, yes. I want the kids to feel as safe as possible."

"Let me know when you're ready and I'll install it, personally."

My eyes widened. "Grandpa, you're far too busy for that. I'm sure some of the mages can –"

"Nonsense. This is the first orphanage in the demon world, built by my granddaughter. I'm going to install it to ensure it's perfect." He winked. "Just like you."

I rolled my eyes at him, but couldn't stop smiling. Having such powerful family members did come in handy.

"Have you and your people discussed installing solar and wind power for electricity?" Grandpa Nico asked Jol.

Jol turned to me. "What do you think? Is it okay to use?"

I nodded. "Both are good solutions to adding power. They will require quite a bit of infrastructure and other work before you can start utilizing it. However, in the end, I think the demons will appreciate having power." I knew I did. "Oh!" I gasped. "We haven't discussed currency." How had I forgotten to bring it up?

"We discussed it previously and agreed that we would

have the demons bring items and sell them here, or work here, to earn our currency," Dad answered. "It seemed easier than the demons creating a currency that they never had before."

"It's going to take our people a bit of time to get used to the knowledge that certain bits of paper and coins will be worth something significant over here," Jol said.

I could understand how they'd see that as strange, especially when they'd been used to a bartering and trading system that didn't involve money.

"Are you ready to go?" Trey asked Jol.

I turned with my brows furrowed. "Are you going somewhere with him?"

"We're taking him out to dinner," Trey explained with a smile. "Wasn't that one of the things you've been wanting to do?"

Squealing, I threw my arms around his neck and kissed him. "Yes! Thank you! Where are we going?"

"Well, we thought we'd start off at a place we're all familiar with," Kayden said. "Brickhouse."

My mouth instantly watered. "Yes, please."

"Are we invited, too?" Mom asked. "You're going to our favorite restaurant, after all."

"That's up to Jol," Trey said. He turned to Jol and asked, "Would you prefer a more intimate experience with just us, or are you okay with taking more people?"

"I think I'd like to experience what Lily would experience if she were to eat there," he said.

"Oh, boy," I mumbled and shook my head. "Now you've done it."

"I already called and reserved the entire restaurant!" Great Aunt Leona announced as she walked into the room.

"I didn't even know you were here," I admitted.

She pouted. "How awfully rude of you, Grand Niece! I was just in the other room."

Rushing over, I hugged her and patted her back. "There, there, Great Auntie. You know how stifling it gets with so many alphas in a room."

She pretended to sniffle and nodded. "There is a lot of alpha testosterone in the air. So, shall we go?"

"How will we get there?" Jol asked. "In that ... car, thing?"

"My good friend," Grandpa Nico said with a smile and set his hand on Jol's shoulder. "We teleport."

"Teleport?" Jol asked with a frown and looked at me.

I waved and smiled wide. "See you there!"

He opened his mouth, but Grandpa Nico winked at me and teleported Jol, Nana Jolie, Great Aunt Leona, and Grandpa Rhys away in the next instant.

"Portal or teleport?" Mom asked me.

"Portal," I said with a nod.

"Yes, thank you," Branson, one of Mom's other mates and another of my adoptive fathers who I called Bran Bran, said.

"Oh, Branny Boy," Mom said with a shake of her head. "I only teleported you somewhere high that made you fall *one* time. Have you so little faith in your mate?"

"They make my stomach queasy," he admitted.

The bear shifter was far from small and hearing him admit that had me snickering and trying to hide it.

"Oh, you think that's funny? Come here, Daughter!" He started chasing me around the room and I laughed as he did.

Mom opened a portal in the wall before me, giving me an escape. I ran through it, right into the dining room area of Brickhouse where Jol was already seated at a large table.

It looked like they'd stuck four or five tables together to give us the largest table possible.

"Hello," I panted as I walked over.

Jol's eyes widened before he looked at the portal behind me. "Ah, a portal. Your family is very powerful."

Sitting next to him, I said, "Honestly, Jol, you don't know the half of it. Had I not asked them to avoid harming the demons, it would not have been a pretty battle."

"Is that a threat?" he asked, arching a brow.

Rolling my eyes, I flicked one of his horns. "Absolutely not."

"How is Elrith settling in?" he asked.

"Really well, actually. He's with my brother and my best friend right now. They're both hybrid shifters and my brother was excited about getting a nephew. Elrith is definitely going to be spoiled."

"I'm glad to know that he will be so well taken care of," Jol said. "Apparently, Talrinir was next in line to adopt him if you hadn't."

"Speaking of Talrinir," I commented. "You two seem closer. Something going on there?"

He shrugged and picked up a fork with a nonchalant expression. "Perhaps."

"She'd make a great queen," Trey said.

A sudden bout of jealousy surged through me, but I quickly tamped it down, knowing it was ridiculous to feel.

Unfortunately, from Trey's smirk, he had felt the emotion through our bond.

"I agree, she would," I said, and cleared my throat.

"Are we having our usual drinks?" the waiter asked.

"Yes!" I shouted, making everyone laugh.

"I'll have whatever Princess Lily is having," Jol said.

"Do we need time to read the menu?"

"No, bring us our usual, plus one of my usual dinners for our friend," Mom said.

"We'll have what Lily is having," Trey said.

"I also need four orders of cheesecake and one of my dinners to go when we leave," I said.

He bowed his head. "As you wish, Princess."

Our drinks were brought out shortly thereafter and Jol sipped at his, eyes widening. "It's bubbly and sweet."

I nodded and sighed happily. "So tasty."

"Did you try out that game?" Nana Jolie asked.

Kayden nodded. "We got sucked into it pretty fast. I think Lily's already maxed out on her skills."

"Not cooking," Mason commented. "She sucks at it."

"That's not very nice to say," Jol said with a scowl.

Smiling, I said, "They're talking about in a videogame, not real life."

"Though, she's not great in real life either," Mason muttered.

My smile disappeared and I kicked his shin, softly, beneath the table. "Rude!"

He smiled and asked, "Remember when you made brownies for my birthday?"

"Those were weapons, not brownies," Bran Bran muttered down the table.

Jol looked confused, so I explained. "I made brownies, which is a chocolate dessert that is supposed to be soft, but I overcooked them and they were super hard."

"They only became weapons because you were rude," Riddick reminded Branson.

"I threw one at his head," I told Jol. "He dodged it."

"Barely," Branson muttered.

"Oh, the chicken pasta was another epic failure," Caleb said.

I gasped. "You said you liked it!"

"We all lied," Mom said.

Nana Jolie fanned her face. "Don't mention it. I barely kept that down."

"You could have told me," I mumbled, embarrassed.

"You should have tried Caleb's first cooking attempt," Nana Jolie said and scoffed.

"It was toxic," Grandpa Rhys said.

"Dubious food," Nana Jolie said with a snicker.

"And none of you taught me how to improve it," Dad shot back. "I had to go to a cooking school."

"You went to a cooking school?" I asked, shocked since I hadn't heard that before.

"After we adopted you," Mom said with a nod. "He wanted to learn to cook so he could make you tasty and healthy meals."

That was the absolute sweetest thing I had heard! My adoptive father, a king, had taken cooking classes for me.

"That's so sweet," I squeaked.

"I think I'd like to take cooking classes," Jol commented.

We all looked at him.

"Really?" I asked.

He nodded. "You have so much variety in your foods. I'd like to learn and also have my people learn, how to use the items to make meals for their families."

"That's a great idea," Great Aunt Leona said. "We could have a class to teach them about the foods, their uses, and how to make easy meals using the resources you currently have."

"Can we sign our mates up for that class?" I asked.

My three mates turned wide eyes on me at the same time my fathers and Jol laughed.

"Challenge accepted," Trey said. "I'm going to make you a meal tomorrow that you'll beg me to make weekly after."

"We should learn some new recipes now that we have Elrith," Mason whispered and tapped his finger on the table in thought. "We need to introduce him to healthy foods early."

"Or he might end up picky like Kayden," Mom teased.

"I'm not picky!" Kayden argued.

"You're the pickiest person at this table," Caleb argued. "Which is saying something since Lily is here."

"I just prefer meat," I countered.

"And sweets," Branson said.

"You're the one who always spoiled her by giving her sweets," Nana Jolie countered.

"He was just trying to win her heart, and he did so with the power of sugar that he carried around in his pocket," Triston said with a smile. He turned to me, his tiger striped hair flopping over one eye. "You'd start crying and he'd pull out a candy from his pocket."

"It was the quickest way to calm her down," Branson countered.

They argued back and forth a bit and Jol leaned over to whisper, "I can see why you turned out the way you did. You have a wonderful family."

I smiled and nodded. "I do have a wonderful family." And now it had grown with the addition of Elrith.

"When do I get to see my great grandson again?" Nana Jolie asked.

"Wait, what?" Great Aunt Leona asked. She looked at me. "Are you pregnant?"

"I adopted a hybrid demon boy," I explained with a smile. "Sorry, I didn't exactly have time to send out announcements yet."

Great Aunt Leona gasped, stood, and walked to Caleb. "Take me to him!"

Laughing, I said, "You can meet him after dinner, Great Auntie. You can give him the cheesecake slice I ordered."

With a resigned sigh, she sat back down. "Very well, I accept your offer."

"So, it is the boy who can shift?" Jol asked.

"Yes," I admitted. "He was worried about telling you."

"It isn't something our kind can do, so I understand his hesitancy. I think you are correct, that he is like you, a hybrid demon. That could be where his shadow powers come from as well." He frowned. "I wonder if he could be related to you, since the shadow power is so rare."

"Related to me?" I asked.

He nodded. "Perhaps your demon parent found a family to raise him, since he looks more demon than hybrid? Perhaps they knew he would face many hardships in this world versus ours."

My brows furrowed as I considered it, but my parents had died when I was Elrith's age.

"What if your missing mother was Third to Reign's daughter, a demoness, and she went back to the demon realm? What if she left you with your hybrid father here, because you lacked horns and demon features, so she knew you would do better here and after returning to the demon realm, she found a new mate who she had Elrith with?" Mason suggested. "It's not unheard of for women to have babies so far apart."

"But, if she was alive so recently, then why did she allow the Grand Advisor to cause such havoc?" I asked. No, I didn't think that made sense. Shaking my head, I said as much.

"It was just a theory," Jol said. "He could be a cousin or some other type of relative."

It was an interesting theory, though. And it made me wonder what had happened to my biological mother.

Shaking my head, I cleared it of the thoughts. It was best not to go down that thought path.

Our food came out, creating the perfect distraction.

CHAPTER
FIFTEEN

"Mama!" Elrith shouted and jumped onto the bed.

I shot upright, looking for what had caused his fear.

"It's alright," Trey said from the doorway where he stood with a towel over one shoulder.

"He's trying to drown me!" Elrith cried and crawled into my lap.

My brain finally caught up to the situation and I pet his hair between his horns, the understanding slow due to my just awakened state. "He's not trying to drown you, Elrith. He's trying to give you a bath, to clean you. It's important to take baths and be clean."

"What?" he tilted his face up, a frown pulling down his cute lips.

"We all wash at least every other day," I explained. "If you don't want to take a bath, you can take a shower. I prefer showers."

"I don't understand," he admitted.

Trey held out his hand. "I'll show you. You can stand next to me in the bathroom while I show you what the water will do and explain the process, okay?"

"Go on," I urged. "Once you're done cleaning yourself, we're going to run some errands and you'll get to see more of this world."

After a moment of hesitation, he crawled out of the bed and walked to Trey, though it was obvious he was still reluctant to do so.

Now awake, I went about changing and freshening up. Downstairs, I could hear Kayden humming as he moved pans and things about, which meant he must be cooking breakfast.

Skipping down the stairs, I almost ran into Kayden who caught me around the waist and spun us in a circle to set my feet on the ground. "Hello, beautiful."

Pressing a quick kiss to his cheek, I smiled at him. "Morning, handsome."

"Breakfast is ready for you. I was on my way up to wake you, but seems our little imp was first to reach you."

"He was scared of bathing," I explained.

Kayden frowned. "Scared of bathing?"

I nodded and stepped out of his arms to go to the kitchen to get my food. "He thought Trey was trying to drown him, apparently."

Kayden laughed. "That had to have hurt his pride."

My brows furrowed, as I hadn't even thought of how that interaction might have upset Trey. I needed to be more aware of my mates' and their feelings. The bonds had randomly opened, surprising all of us as we'd been relaxing and watching a movie. I'd locked down the bonds pretty tight in order to sleep last night, so I hadn't felt Trey's emotion this morning.

Opening them now, I felt happiness from him, so Elrith must have stopped being scared.

"How are you feeling?" Mason asked as he made his plate next to me.

"Fine," I replied immediately.

He scowled at me. "Lily."

"Honestly?" I asked and looked up at him. "I'm still weak. I can't seem to recharge fully and definitely not as quickly as I can in the demon world."

"We could go back until you feel better," he suggested, concern making his brows furrow.

The desire to go back was strong, but I didn't want to make that decision yet. I knew Trey wasn't as on board about moving there as Mason was.

I wasn't sure what Kayden felt about the possibility of us living there, either. His dad was here, after all.

"I'm fine for now," I said. "We have things to do here."

"It's a discussion we need to have," Mason whispered and pressed a kiss to the top of my head. "And you recuperating fully is the most important thing right now."

"Right now, I want to focus on Elrith," I said and headed to the table to eat.

Elrith and Trey joined us shortly after, Elrith wearing baggy clothes, which solidified my plan to take him shopping today.

When everyone had finished eating, we climbed into Kayden's SUV and headed to the mall.

Elrith pressed his nose against the window, staring with

wide eyes at everything we drove by. When a dragon flew by overhead, he gasped and cowered down.

I set a hand on his back and said, "You don't need to fear a dragon flying overhead."

He raised his head slowly. "No?"

"They're part of my clan," Trey said. "I'm a dragon prince and as my son, they won't harm you or they know they'll face not just my wrath, but my family's as well."

Yet, that wasn't fully true, was it? I'd been attacked and so had he, just for being part of the royal family.

Trey glanced at me with a frown.

Had my emotions leaked through the bond? Whoops.

"We are taking you to a place that will have a lot of people, so I need you to stay close to us, so you don't get lost. Okay?"

Elrith looked back at me. "What are we doing there?"

"We're going to buy you some clothes and other items that you need," Mason explained.

"What's wrong with my clothes?" he asked and looked down.

"Those don't fit you and you need several different outfits," I answered.

"Okay," he replied and looked back out the window.

Honestly, he was handling all this much better than I had anticipated. He'd been curious about the cars, but hadn't freaked out like I'd expected.

After parking, Trey got a call and held up his hand to stop us from exiting the vehicle. "Yes?" With a sigh, he asked, "Really? You know ... fine. Fine." He hung up, irritation obvious, but he smiled as he said, "Looks like we'll have a friend with us on this shopping trip."

My eyes widened as I realized what must have happened. "Who?"

"Ezio," Trey answered.

Kayden's brows furrowed. "Why didn't he call me?"

"It was Caleb who called to inform me," Trey said. He glanced over at Elrith. "Apparently, they wanted him to tag along, just in case."

"He's probably also mad that we haven't visited him or introduced him to Elrith," I whispered.

Kayden flinched. "Yeah, that's most likely why he is the one here."

"Well, let's not keep him waiting! Elrith, you're going to get to meet one of your other grandpas, Ezio is Kayden's dad."

His eyes widened as he looked at Kayden. "Your dad?"

Kayden nodded. "He's a strong werewolf. In fact, he used to be Lily's guard."

Elrith turned to me. "You had a guard?"

I nodded. "Most of my life Ezio would go with me places and keep me safe. He's very strong, though, a bit older now."

Trey opened the door for us and I took Elrith's hand after stepping out.

"Is crashing your shopping trips the only way I'll get to see you four?" Ezio asked as he walked up to us.

"You know where we live," Trey reminded him.

"It's good to see you," I said and hugged him.

He squeezed me tight and pushed me back to give me a stern glare. "Can you not follow in the footsteps of your mom and Jolie by endangering yourself for the world? My heart isn't as young as it once was and when I saw what was happening, I nearly had a heart attack."

"Don't worry, that's my one and only sacrificial moment." I held my hand with three fingers up. "Promise."

Especially since I didn't have the power to do it again, not that he needed to know that bit of information.

Kayden picked up Elrith and held him with Elrith's legs wrapped around his stomach. "Pop, meet our imp, Elrith. Elrith, this is Grandpa Ezio," Kayden introduced.

"Imp?" Ezio whispered, but quickly smiled and took a step closer to them. "Hello, Elrith. You've got very nice horns."

Elrith preened. "They're pretty large for my age. Even the king praised them."

Putting my hand over my mouth, I hid my smile and snicker. He was so cute.

"Shall we go shopping? I hear you need some clothes and necessities," Ezio said and turned to head inside.

"What does he shift into?" Elrith whispered to Kayden.

"A wolf," I answered. "He can also take a warrior shift, like my dad."

"Well, similar," Ezio said. "Caleb's always been a bit ... special."

"As expected of the only purebred hybrid," I said with a shrug.

"Right," Ezio said with a nod.

"Does it hurt you to shift?" he asked.

Ezio shook his head. "No. What about you, imp? Does shifting hurt you?"

Elrith shook his head. "The shadow protects me."

Ezio raised his brows. "That's good to hear." He looked at me. "Shadow seems to run in the family."

We stepped into the mall and were immediately bombarded by media.

Elrith gasped as the cameras flashed their bright lights and the reporters began shouting questions, and ducked his head into Kayden's chest.

Trey stepped forward and shouted, "That's enough!"

The reporters silenced and stopped taking pictures.

"You should be calling for an official request for interview, not bombarding them this way," Ezio growled as he had stepped up as well. "You're frightening my grandchild and I won't have that!" His alpha aura exploded outwards, knocking the reporters who weren't human back two steps.

"Deep breath," Mason whispered as he set a hand on my lower back.

I looked over at him and obeyed, quickly realizing that I had shifted into warrior form at the gasp from Elrith. Closing my eyes, I took a deep breath and relaxed, shifting back to human. "Whoops."

"Mama," Elrith whined.

Kayden handed him to me, and my three mates formed a triangle of protection, with Elrith hidden between them.

"It's alright," I whispered as I rubbed his back. "They're not bad people, just loud and bright."

"Not danger?" he asked and peeked up at me from his lashes.

I smiled. "Not a danger."

"You shifted," he commented.

Nodding, I admitted, "It was a reaction to your fear and the loud noises."

"Mama got a bit overprotective just now," Mason whispered.

"Hopefully, now she understands why we do it to her," Trey muttered as we walked through the reporters who had stepped aside to allow us entry.

Perhaps we should have brought guards with us after all, but I'd given them the day off to spend time with their families.

"Clothing store first?" Ezio asked.

"Yes," I replied.

Now that he knew there was no danger, Elrith sat up and looked around, his eyes wide and mouth open.

A little girl with silver hair and slitted pupils waved at us. "Hi, Princess!"

I waved back. "Hello!"

"She knows you?" Elrith asked.

"Everyone knows her," Ezio answered. "She's the hybrid princess who can shift into a giant snake, after all."

"There aren't many shake shifters," I added. "That little girl is one, too, judging by her slitted pupils."

"She must get picked on," Elrith said with a scowl. He looked up at me. "Did you get picked on?"

"No," Mason said immediately. "We made sure to protect her when we were young."

They had beat up quite a few kids, mostly purebred shifters who hated us for being hybrids anyways, and hated me more for being a snake.

"Good," Elrith whispered. He looked back over my shoulder. "I hope she has someone to protect her."

I had a feeling this boy was going to be a lady killer like his adoptive fathers.

"Are you going to put him in the hybrid school or the main school?" Ezio asked as we entered the children's clothing store.

"Hybrid," I answered at the same time Trey said, "Main."

We looked at each other, eyes wide.

"You can't seriously think we can send him to the main school?" Mason said.

"He *needs* to go to the main school, like Caleb did, to prove his rightful place is among the population," Kayden countered.

Oh, boy. Seems we were divided equally about this issue.

"Obviously, you four have to discuss it more," Ezio said with a smirk.

Truthfully, I still wanted to move to the demon world.

"We can discuss it later," I said and set Elrith down to start picking out clothes. "If you see clothes you want to try on, just let one of us know," I told him.

His eyes widened. "I can try on whatever I want?"

"Yes," Trey answered. "Any of these that you want."

"Hello, friends," a pretty elven woman greeted us, a nametag on her shirt with "Claire" on it.

"Hello, Claire," I greeted. "The little prince here is in need of some new clothes."

She smiled at Elrith, who had hidden behind Mason at her approach. "Wonderful! Let me know if there's anything specific you are looking for that you don't see here. We can order many things."

"What about shirts for wings?" Trey asked.

"Right this way, Prince Trey," she said, bowed, and lead him over to a section marked for dragons.

"Go on," I urged Elrith. "Go with them."

Mason nudged him forward with a nod and he quickly jogged over to grip onto Trey's shirt hem.

After grabbing several different types of shirts and pants, I headed over to the dressing rooms and put them inside one of the empty ones.

Trey and Elrith joined us, their arms full of clothes as well, but from Elrith's wide smile, he didn't seem to mind that he'd have to try them all on.

An hour later, we'd purchased an entirely new wardrobe for him.

"Shopping is fun!" Elrith gasped. "I'm thirsty, though."

"Let's stop in the food court before we go to the other stores," I suggested. "I'm a bit thirsty myself."

Mason found a table for us and pulled out my chair for me. I kissed him on the cheek as I sat and looked at Trey and Kayden as I said, "See? Romantic."

Mason smiled smugly and sat beside me, reaching over to entwine our fingers together.

"What do you want to drink?" Kayden asked.

"A lemonade," Ezio answered and scoffed. "No wonder she's pointing out how unromantic you are, you don't even know what she likes to drink here." Ezio held out his hand. "Come on, Elrith. Let's get you a snack and your mama a drink."

Elrith glanced at Kayden, who nodded, and he quickly took Ezio's hand and let him lead him to the line for my favorite lemonade place.

"Cookie!" I shouted.

Ezio held up a hand with his thumb up without turning around to let me know he'd heard.

"It's not my fault I don't know what you like here," Kayden muttered and folded his arms over his chest. "Dad took you out and Mom wouldn't let me go most times."

"I'm still convinced she secretly dislikes me," I whispered, and Mason squeezed my hand.

"She hates me, too, it's okay," Trey said.

"That's just because you've always been such a cocky brat," Mason said.

Trey scowled. "Excuse you?"

"He's not wrong. You often acted spoiled around Mom," Kayden agreed.

"He acted like that because she made him nervous," I said.

All three turned to me.

"How'd you know that?" Trey asked. "I've never told anyone that."

Smiling, I leaned forward and said, "Mate, I've known you most of your life. I could tell whenever you were around her that you'd get tense and your responses were always clipped. She thought you were being conceited or that you thought you were better than her, but I knew it was because she scared you."

"Scared you? My mom is super sweet," Kayden argued.

"She was sweet to you," I countered. "She yelled at us when you weren't nearby."

His eyes widened. "She what?"

"Actually, she told me I should keep away from you after we graduated. When I told her I was going away for college, she actually breathed out in relief." I shrugged. "Not sure why she doesn't like me, but she's never wanted us to end up together."

Kayden scowled and sat back in his chair. "I'm going to have to talk to her about that."

I waved it away. "It doesn't matter now. You're mine and she can't change that. There's no need to bring it up."

I was fairly certain it was her concern over the spell I'd taken for Mom when we were on the island. And that Kayden wouldn't look at other girls when I was around.

"Why didn't you ever tell me?" Kayden asked with a frown.

I shrugged and said, "Because there's not much you could do. Plus, I hoped as I grew and changed that she would learn to like me. When we stopped talking, she was nicer to me whenever she saw me, but I bet now that we're mates, she'll go back to being annoyed by me."

"I'll talk to her," Kayden whispered.

"It's okay, Trey's mom hates me even more."

Trey sighed. "She doesn't like *me* most days."

"No, she's always been pissed that you spend your time with us, sullying your pure-blooded-ness with us hybrids," Mason countered. "She tried to threaten me into stopping our friendship when we were teens."

"Same," Kayden said with a nod.

Trey blinked in stunned silence.

"Well, anyway, I'm glad we have family who does approve," I said, and looked over at Ezio, who was talking to Elrith, both smiling wide.

No matter what their moms thought, their sons were mine now, so they'd just have to accept me. That thought made me smile, earning curious stares from my mates.

SIXTEEN

The days passed so quickly and quietly that I didn't realize how *many* had passed until I looked at the date.

The orphanage was well under construction and all of the other updates and plans were going into effect. The public opinion was varied, but many were embracing the trade options and hiring the demons who requested work here. We had announced our adoption of Elrith as well. The poor little guy had hated all the posing for pictures, but he loved looking at them afterwards.

I still wasn't recuperated, but Trey had been dealing with something with the dragons that kept taking him from home, so we hadn't yet returned to the demon world. It was one of a handful of topics we needed to discuss.

"Mama, can we go tour the school soon?" Elrith asked softly.

"Your fathers and I still have to discuss school. I think you're better suited for a school in the demon world," I replied.

Elrith sat on the couch next to me, eyes glued to the TV as we watched the news.

"I want to learn about this world," he whispered. "There's so much I don't know."

He was right that we needed to decide. We had to register him soon.

"When Trey and Mason return, I'll talk to them, okay?"

He nodded and resumed focusing on the news.

Kayden walked in with a tray of snacks and juice boxes. "We do have a long discussion ahead of us."

Understatement of the year.

The doorbell rang, and Kayden and I looked at each other with matching frowns. "I'll go see who it is," he said and quickly left.

Not even a minute later, Trey's mother barged into the living room. She was a pretty woman, in her late fifties with black hair that was slowly greying at her temple; the greying made her look even more distinguished. Today she wore a blue silk dress that made me think of the ocean for some reason. However, her pretty face was a façade for the vile temper that simmered in her chest. "What do you have to say for yourself?" she snapped at me, hands on her hips.

My eyes widened at her abrupt tone. "What?"

"Was it your demon powers? Is that how you bewitched Trey? He is the smartest of the dragon males. How did you do it?" She snapped. Her eyes darted to Elrith, who had scooted across the couch to hide behind me. "And you convinced him to adopt this ... thing?"

Shooting to my feet, I marched up to her, snarling, and knew I had partially shifted. "You cannot barge into my house and insult me and my son like this! Your son is not bewitched. He loves me and I love him. Just because you've never approved of hybrids, doesn't mean your son shares your archaic beliefs. You could learn many things from him if you weren't so stubborn and continued to stick to outdated beliefs."

She scoffed and folded her arms across her chest. "Learn from him? I would never mate with trash like you or pick up litter from another world. You're nothing, but a conceited trollop and that *thing* you call a son is—"

My hand swung out on its own, slapping her across the face before I realized what I was doing. A bright red mark spread instantly.

"Get out of my house, you aren't welcome here," I hissed.

She spun on her heels with a harumph and waltzed out without another word. Had that been a smirk on her face I'd seen just before she left, or had I imagined it?

Kayden made sure the door locked before rushing back to me. "Lily—"

I put my face in my hands and whispered, "I'm sorry. I shouldn't have slapped her, but I couldn't stop myself. She ... she ..."

"She deserved it," Kayden said immediately. He turned to Elrith and picked him up, patting his back. "You forget everything that mean, old lady said. She hates everyone and nothing she said is true. Okay?"

He nodded and clung to Kayden, burying his face against his chest.

My phone rang just as we'd gotten resituated on the couch. "Hello?"

"Did you hit my mother?" Trey snapped.

"Y-Yes," I admitted. "She—"

"Why would you hit her, Lily? She may be a thorn in my side and say things that irritate me, but she is still my mother and a dragon princess."

"You don't understand—" I started, but he interrupted me again. My heart began to beat faster, pain coursing through me.

"Is this about me being so busy? If you're upset that I've been gone so much you should just tell me, not take it out on someone else."

Was he taking her side right now without even knowing what happened? My throat constricted as unbidden tears grew in my eyes. "Trey, it's not—"

"I have to go clean up this mess you made. I don't know when I'll be home."

Blinding fury surged within me and my hair flared into rainbows.

"Don't bother," I snapped and stood.

"What?" he asked, worry filtering down the bond.

"Don't bother worrying about when you'll be home because I won't be here," I hissed, my pain and anger merged stronger together and my hair glowed so bright it was like noon in the house despite it being dark outside. "I am your *mate*, but you seem to have forgotten that. Forgotten that you should listen to me and hear out my side of things." I wanted to break something, tear it apart. It was likely the spell ... or perhaps it really was just me. Maybe I did seek pain and destruction.

"Lily, I—"

I hung up and threw my phone into the fireplace.

Elrith and Kayden watched me with matching shocked expressions.

"We're going to the demon world," I informed them. "Go pack."

"Trey and Mason—" Kayden began, but I cut him a glare that had him clamping his lips shut.

We packed our bags, drove to my parents', and Mom teleported me without question, likely because my hair was still glowing and I could barely speak.

I felt Trey touch our bond and threw up the strongest walls I could, dampening the bond until it was nearly severed in my haste.

Perhaps I'd feel bad later, but not now. Not when he'd been so callous.

Talrinir spotted us first, waving from the castle entrance with a wide smile that slowly wilted when she got closer to me. "Princess," she whispered and took one of my hands.

I hadn't realized it, but as soon as I'd put the walls up around Trey and my bond, tears began to stream down my face.

Kayden set a hand on my shoulder, giving me his support and comfort.

"I need to recharge," I gasped out, my chest constricting tighter and tighter. It was like a vice around my body.

She nodded and silently lead the way to the house that the demons had built for me. House was a poor description. Castle was more appropriate. It had ten rooms, a throne room, a spacious living room connected to the kitchen, and a ton of other amenities.

Once inside, I went straight to my room and locked myself inside, laying on my bed and letting the tears fully flow.

After all this time, how could he not know that I wouldn't have touched her had she not spouted vile things? How could he not trust that although I was sorry, it was his mother at fault?

Sometime later, Kayden knocked on the door. "Lily, I put some food and water here for you. Take as much time as you need to recharge."

"Elrith?" I asked.

"Druth came by and picked him up to take him to their city so he could learn a few things. He said to tell you to rest and he'll learn as much as he can while we are here so he can help in the future."

Was I wrong? Had I overreacted? Trey's accusation hurt a lot, though. He should know me and know I wouldn't just hit his mother for no reason.

Should I apologize to her?

The thought of apologizing to that awful woman had my lip curling. No, I wouldn't apologize after she'd said such hurtful things.

Getting out of bed, I opened one of my windows, shifted into snake form, and climbed out. Once outside, beneath the stars, I curled up and relaxed. The energy in the demon world began to fill me, cooling my temper and easing my worry.

I felt Mason tap our bond and tapped it back to let him know I was okay. He was a worrywart after all.

Kayden peeked out the window sometime later, but left me alone.

As the sun rose the next morning, I shifted back into human form and joined Kayden for breakfast.

He kissed the side of my head as he set a plate of cut up fruits and a cooked potato before me. "Options are limited since we haven't been staying here. I'll go into town later to get better food."

I nodded, staying silent as I ate my food.

Kayden set his hand on mine, drawing my gaze. "I'm sorry he treated you that way. I know it may not feel like it now, but once he realizes what a moron he is, you'll work things out."

We were mates, and I loved him immensely, so it wasn't like I was going to throw away all that over this. However, he had some serious groveling ahead of him if he wanted to repair the hurt I felt now.

"He and Mason are on their way," he advised after a moment of silence.

Sighing loudly, I pushed my half-eaten plate away and stood. "I'm going to shower. Sleeping outside left a fine layer of dirt on me."

Kayden nodded. "Take your time. I hear King Rhys helped with the final designs and some additions of this place, which included an upgraded bathroom."

If Grandpa Rhys helped, I'm sure I would love the bathroom.

I placed a quick kiss on his cheek as I walked by. "Thank you for being understanding."

"I'm just glad it wasn't me this time," he whispered so softly I was certain he hadn't meant for me to hear it.

CHAPTER
SEVENTEEN

After finishing my shower in the incredible bathroom, I was surprised to find some beautiful dresses already hanging in my closet.

The material was unlike anything I had seen, let alone worn before, soft and buttery, yet warm. Was it a type of material they made here in the demon world? I picked out a black dress with silver designs that reminded me of snake scales, brushed out my hair, and headed to the living room, where I could feel Mason and Kayden.

As I expected, Trey was seated with them as well, my inability to sense him due to the walls I'd erected around our bond.

He immediately stood when I entered, eyes tracing over me before dropping to the ground. Thick, dark bags hung beneath his eyes and his shoulders hunched forward. "Lily –" he whispered.

"We have a lot to discuss today," I announced. "Starting

with my desire to live in the demon world, here in this castle that they built for me ... for us."

Trey's head whipped up and his eyes widened in surprise. "What?" he whispered.

I sat in a highbacked chair that was at the end of the living room, just before a fireplace that had a roaring fire going. On the mantle above the fireplace, I noticed protection charms had been placed there. Was it one of the builders or one of my friends who'd put the charms there? Even in my foul mood, they made me feel a little lighter. The highbacked chair seemed to mold around me and I relaxed into the comfort of it, letting it help bolster my determination.

Was Trey really so surprised by my desire to live here? Did he not realize how much better I was here? Kayden and Mason noticed. They both understood. Perhaps his hesitation was more to do with the duties he was bound to as royalty.

"I know you will need to travel to the other world to help the dragons and attend to your duties as a dragon prince," I went on. "However, I have a lot that I still want to do here and that world's only appeal to me is the people I love who live there. People I can visit. This world ... this is where I belong. I feel ten times better after just one night here. I just *feel* right here. Plus, I'm so much safer here. Elrith is so much safer here. And, I won't ever have to deal with an *incident* like yesterday while I'm here." Mainly because she would never receive clearance to enter this world. The last sentence came out a little harsher and angrier than I intended, but I wasn't going to apologize for that.

Trey dropped to his knees before me, taking my hands from my lap and holding them in his. Pain rippled across his face as he looked up at me. Pain and regret. "I'm sorry. I should have known better than to listen to her and take what she said at face value, but she called me crying and showed me the red mark on her face and gave me a sob story. I was dealing with some stupidity among my cousins, so I was already upset and I didn't think before reacting." Squeezing my hands, he looked deep into my eyes and said, "I'm sorry, Lily. Truly. I've completely cut her off, and even my father has decided this stunt was the last straw and is discussing separation. I'll do anything you want to prove my sincerity."

I didn't doubt his sincerity. I didn't doubt he felt bad for his mother causing issues between us. That wasn't the point.

"Do you have any argument against living here?" I asked, ignoring his apologies ... for now.

His hands flexed around mine, some emotion I couldn't place flitting across his face before he shook his head. "No, I am agreeable to living here as long as you understand there might be nights that I have to stay over to deal with dragon drama."

"I'd also like Elrith to go to school here until at least middle school. Once he's in middle school, we can then discuss having him attend school at the one we attended, as well as our high school. I agree with you all that he needs to become accustomed to that world and the people there, and the people of that world need to become accustomed to demons as well, but I don't want his first school experiences to be marred by the inevitable harassment he will receive." It wasn't so much the kids I was worried about, but the parents.

"You've really thought this through, huh?" Kayden asked with a proud smirk.

I didn't need to answer him, since he knew the answer already.

"I fully agree," Mason said and Trey nodded his agreement as well.

"I have a favor to ask of you," I said to Trey. Truthfully, what I wanted could be handled by Grandpa Rhys, but I knew it would help heal the rift between Trey and I if I asked him to handle it instead.

"Anything for you," he whispered and rubbed his thumb over my knuckles.

"I want you to find a teacher from the dragons, someone who can teach Elrith about dragon history and about fighting like a dragon shifter. I know he isn't a dragon, but his scales and wings remind me of you when you were his age." And his spirit.

Trey frowned. "And why can't I be that teacher?"

"Because you don't remember shit about dragon history," Mason said. When Trey shot him a dirty look, Mason shrugged a shoulder and asked, "Am I wrong?"

Trey sighed softly and shook his head. "No, you're right." He looked up at me again and nodded. "I'll find a suitable teacher, one who is willing to travel here."

I smiled and squeezed his hands. "Great."

"Anything else we need to discuss?" Mason asked.

All of my other topics weren't ones we needed agreement on, just brainstorming, so I shook my head. Plus, I was exhausted again and ready to relax.

Mason stood, walked over, picked me up, and carried me out of the room.

"What are you doing?" Trey demanded.

He looked over his shoulder and said, "Taking my mate to my room. You haven't graveled enough to join us. Maybe tomorrow. We'll see how you do."

I hid my smirk against his chest even though I knew Mason could sense my amusement.

"Wait!" Trey shouted, desperation in his voice that had Mason turning around so I could face him. His pinched face concerned me. "Can you please, please, unblock our bond?" he begged. "It's ... I feel hollow, empty, and in so much pain. I can't ... I can't survive another night separated from you physically *and* through the bond."

I immediately released the bond and he staggered to his knees in relief.

Mason nodded, turned, and resumed carrying me to our room. "I wouldn't have done it if I were you. I'd have made him suffer some more." There was a bit of growl to his voice and when I focused on him, I realized he was mad at Trey.

"He's sorry, I can tell he truly is, otherwise I would have left it blocked," I said.

Mason set me on the bed in the room that was his before shutting the door and turning around to face me with a frown on his handsome face.

I held out my hand to him. "I'm sorry you were caught in the crossfire and had to spend a night away from me."

He kicked his shoes off, removed his pants and shirt, and crawled onto the bed in only his boxers, quickly curling around me.

Resting my head on his bare chest, I inhaled his scent and relaxed as I listened to the steady beat of his heart.

Gripping my knee, he pulled it over his legs so I lay across him and we both exhaled a sigh of relief.

"I understand why you left. As soon as I realized what had happened, I laid into Trey, but it was too late. You needed to come here to recharge anyways, we'd discussed it several times, so I wasn't surprised this is where you went. I just wish Kayden had been with him instead of me, so I could have accompanied you here. I felt your pain, and it took a lot of control not to beat sense into Trey with my fists. His mother called him crying and hysterical, claiming you'd attacked her in front of Elrith and making crazy statements. I'd rolled my eyes, knowing she was lying, but Trey was stressed from his stupid cousins and reacted extremely poorly. Not that it's an excuse, just what happened."

"What did his cousins do?" I asked as I traced the snake scales on his tattoo with my fingertip.

"One of them impregnated a human girl, barely eighteen, who was engaged to an elf. The elf and he had some history and he'd done it out of spite, not thinking about the conse-quences."

I gasped. "That poor girl!"

He nodded, his cheek rubbing against the top of my head from the movement. "Trey ensured she's going to be taken care of by his cousin. No matter what the reason, that's his child and his responsibility. Then, one of his other cousins stole something from the mana stone store. He made that cousin return it and apologize to your parents. He hates hybrids, so it was a pain to get him to relent and just apolo-gize instead of facing more serious consequences."

"I bet Grandpa Rhys was rubbing his temples from a

headache over all this," I whispered and smiled slightly as I pictured the scene.

"He wasn't available, that's part of why Trey was handling it. Some emergency in the mage lands that King Nico needed help with."

Grandpa Nico needing help? That seemed incredibly unlikely. Then again, there was always some craziness happening in our worlds. You couldn't have magical creatures of so many types living together without issue.

He blew out a breath and squeezed me tight. "It was still completely ridiculous of him to call you and say what he said. I knew she was being her typical dramatic self, but ... anyway. I'm glad to be back with you."

"Me too." Squeezing tighter against him, we held each other for a long time, just basking in each other's company.

"I'm excited to see everything that you're planning. I know you've got a lot you didn't talk about tonight. I could see it in your eyes."

Laughing, I tilted my head back to look up at him. "You could?"

He tucked hair behind my ear and smiled, my heart racing a bit faster. "Yes. Also, I have some ideas I wanted to discuss, too."

"Now?"

Chuckling, he shook his head. "No, beautiful. Now, we relax, eat some snacks I'll sneak in here, and then sleep. You're feeling better, I can tell, but you're still not fully recovered. You still need rest and relaxation. So, put your head down and let me protect you as you sleep tonight."

"Bossy," I hissed, though I agreed. I knew without a doubt

that I'd sleep like a rock tonight and that the likelihood of attack was extremely low here, but with him, Kayden, and Trey here as well, I was safe.

We told each other stories from our time apart, snacked on random treats he'd brought with him, and then curled up together beneath the covers when the sun set.

My thoughts began drifting, and within minutes I fell into a deep, dreamless sleep.

AFTER A DELICIOUS BREAKFAST made by Kayden, Mason, Kayden, and I gathered in the living room and started our brainstorming.

"Here's my suggestion," Mason began. "We should offer field trips for the orphanages to go to the other world, to learn about both places and to help with developing relationships between them. If we start the kids off as friends from a young age, when they reach middle school, they're far less likely to have issues attending the same school together. I really like your idea of the kids staying in their worlds for elementary school, then going to middle school and high school together. Plus, that means we won't have to build additional middle schools and high schools here."

I gasped. "I love that idea! The kids can play together and it could lead to more adoption opportunities for those willing to adopt from the other world."

Trey joined us, a stack of papers in his hands. His

normally styled hair was a mess and bags hung beneath his eyes.

I had released our bond, which I quickly double checked, so why was he so sleep deprived?

"I found an instructor for Elrith," he stated before putting a hand over his mouth to stifle a yawn. "I also came up with this." He pressed a kiss to my temple before setting the papers on the coffee table before me.

I grabbed his arm, stilling him. "Why're you so tired? I opened the bond and—"

He smiled and squatted down in front of me. "My lack of sleep was due to calls, emails, and planning. Not you, love." Leaning up, he rubbed his cheek against mine, making a purring sound. "I was excited by my idea."

I rested my hand against his face, and he immediately leaned into it with a sigh of contentment. "Eat while I read your idea," I ordered.

His eyes flashed, but instead of a snippy retort, he turned his head and kissed my palm. "As my goddess wishes."

After watching him a moment to ensure he went to the kitchen and followed my orders, I pulled his papers into my lap to read them. My eyes widened, and I gasped at what I read. "You created an entire curriculum that incorporates both worlds' history and defensive training for the kids in one night?"

"It's just an outline," he mumbled around the breakfast burrito he'd taken a bite of. "This is delicious, Kayden." He turned back to me. "I need to talk to Druth or Talrinir to get more information from them before I can expand the curriculum fully. I'm not quite sure what they teach the kids here, and I don't want to assume."

"Speaking of them, when will Elrith be home?" I asked. I missed the little imp and his cuddles. The poor thing was seemingly touch starved, but with four of us, we were doing our best to fix that ... and probably spoiling him in the process. A process I was a-okay with as I also enjoyed all the extra cuddles.

The front door flew open and Elrith yelled, "I'm home!"

"Speak of the little devil," Mason said with a smile as he stood.

I leaped to my feet and raced to the door, beating them all, scooped up Elrtih, and hugged him tight. "Elrith!"

He giggled as I nuzzled his cheek. "Mama!"

My heart soared. I was certain I would never tire of hearing him call me that. I also knew to treasure it while it happened because once he became a teenager, all bets were off on what he'd call me.

"Nice to see where we rank on greetings," Jol whispered.

My head snapped up, and I gasped at him and Talrinir. "Sorry!" It was actually a bad sign that I hadn't even paid attention to who else was here besides Elrith.

They both smiled, seeming to understand my lack of etiquette.

Talrinir wrapped her arms around both me and Elrith. "Hello, friend."

"Fur is tickly," Elrith giggled.

Her furred ears were soft.

Jol hugged the three of us, earning a growl from Mason.

Jol and I looked at each other and rolled our eyes simultaneously as he stepped back.

Elrith leapt from my arms to Mason's, causing him to pause and refocus his attention. "Is there food, Papa?"

Mason's eyes softened even more, and he nodded. "Kayden made burritos. Let's each get one before Trey eats them all."

"I've only had three," Trey grunted, making Mason and Elrith laugh.

Turning back to Jol and Talrinir, my eyes dropped to their now joined hands. A smile split my face and I rushed forward to hug them both. "Congratulations!"

Talrinir laughed, pure joy lighting up her face and Jol patted my back and said, "Thank you."

"Huh? What'd we miss?" Kayden asked from the kitchen.

"King Jolmach and I are ... courting," Talrinir explained.

Kayden rushed over and high-fived Jol. "Congrats, man!"

Jol smiled down at Talrinir. "I'm very fortunate that she is allowing me this chance."

"Is that why you brought Elrith instead of asking us to pick him up?" I asked. "So you could tell us?"

Talrinir nodded. "That and to check on you, but you look one hundred times better. Have you decided about staying here yet? Our world definitely agrees with you."

I opened my mouth, but Trey interrupted me.

"We will be living here permanently," he advised them.

Talrinir barked, a sound I hadn't heard from her before, and pulled me into a tight hug. "I'm so glad! We'll be able to spend more time together."

"And I'll be able to help with your wedding planning," I replied with a wink.

Her cheeks flushed and she self-consciously stroked one of her doglike ears. "Eh, hm, yes."

"I've got a lot of plans in the works," I informed them. "Some we will need your and Druth's help for."

She smiled warmly and said, "I can't wait to hear about them. We have plans today, but how about tomorrow?"

I nodded. "Perfect! Have fun tonight and we'll come to the castle for lunch tomorrow."

Jol smirked. "For lunch, huh? I guess I'll have to make sure we have extra rolls for a certain little imp."

Elrith gasped. "You give another imp extra rolls?"

We all laughed at his outrage, and at his confusion, we all laughed harder.

CHAPTER
EIGHTEEN

The sun had barely peeked through the curtains when an immensely strong aura drew near us. One that felt powerful and ... somewhat familiar.

Elrith raced into the kitchen where Trey and I were finishing making breakfast, his eyes wide with fear, and leapt into Trey's arms, shaking.

"What is it?" Trey asked him.

Mason and Kayden hurried from their rooms, headed to the front door to go face whoever or whatever it was.

I joined them, pushing open the door and stepping out first, ignoring Kayden's soft growl.

The hairs on my nape rose at the sight of a pack of at least a dozen hellhounds jogging towards us.

No wonder Elrith had been scared.

At the front of the pack was a familiar, but much larger than I remembered, hellhound.

"Dhun!" I yelled and ran forward, arms spread wide to hug him.

He yipped in greeting before letting his tongue loll out the side of his mouth in a hellhound grin. He picked up speed and ran forward to meet me.

However, instead of hugging the quilled body of a hellhound, I ended up with my arms around a six foot tall, fleshy, humanoid male.

Jerking backwards from him, I blinked in shock as I stared into the familiar eyes of Dhun, in what appeared to be a human male's body. His skin was dark with darker toned swirling tattoos along his arms and neck that looked like thorns, and his hair was made of a combination of hair and quills, both black and sparkling in the sunrise.

"Hello, Princess!" he greeted me with a warm smile. "Sorry my new appearance startled you."

"Not just your appearance, but your power as well," Mason commented from just behind me.

I flinched, not realizing Mason had moved to my shoulder, likely when Dhun had transformed.

Dhun smiled at Mason. "Yes, it seems I've gained a few bonus perks in my new role."

"New role?" I asked.

He nodded and smiled even wider as he announced, "I'm pack leader of the hellhounds!" The gathered hellhounds howled and yipped excitedly. "Now, I have more powers including being able to shift into this form to easily communicate with others to help with the advancement of our kind."

"I thought demons didn't differentiate between themselves?" Kayden asked from my other shoulder.

Had they both run up when Dhun had shifted forms? Or had they just followed me and I hadn't noticed.

Dhun shrugged. "Me neither, yet I was given the mantle and here I am."

"Given the mantle by who?" Mason asked.

He looked at me and said, "Princess Liliana, of course! When she called me from the other world to help."

How could that be possible? I didn't know how to give people powers or anything like that! Plus, I hadn't purposefully called him. I'd sent Azgon to free him, but ... maybe I'd done it subconsciously. Maybe it was part of my powers as princess and Third to Reign's heir?

"You seem shocked, though, I suppose that makes sense. It was shocking to me when I shifted for the first time as well." He laughed and shook his head.

"Mama! Are ... are you safe?" Elrith called from the doorway where he still clung to Trey, little body shaking hard and eyes wide in terror.

Dhun's face softened as he faced Elrith. Shocking us all, he walked forward a few steps before dropping to a knee and bowing his head. "Greetings, Prince Elrith. I am Dhun, pack leader of the hellhounds. I offer you my sincerest and most heartfelt sympathies for the loss of your blood parents." He raised his eyes to meet Elrith's and continued, "We have punished the ones who killed them. Your mother and father's souls are released and those who harmed them will never harm another."

Elrith stopped shaking and tears sprung to his eyes. "Y-You killed them?"

Dhun nodded. "We will not tolerate unnecessary killings amongst our people. All of the hellhounds have been instructed as such. They also know that Princess Liliana, her mates, you as her son, and all her family are to be protected at all costs. If you ever need me, you only need to howl and I will race to your rescue."

Elrith patted Trey on the shoulder and he set Elrith down. Taking slow steps, Elrith walked to Dhun and said, "Thank you."

Dhun smiled at Elrith and said, "I also bring a gift for my apology to show our sincerity."

My eyebrows shot up into my hairline as a hellhound pup close in size to Elrith trotted forward to sit beside Dhun. The pup looked up at Elrith with their tongue lolled out the side of their mouth.

"This is my daughter, Kora. She is your guard, assigned to stay by your side and protect you, no matter what world you may go to. She will learn how to fight from us, a shared mental bond we have, and will alert us if there is need for our additional aid."

He was giving us his daughter?! While it was normal for a guard to be assigned to royalty, like Ezio had been mine, I hadn't anticipated Elrith's first guard being a hellhound pup, especially not Dhun's child.

"Are you certain of this?" I asked Dhun.

He smiled at me over his shoulder and nodded once. "Yes. She will be a good guard and friend to Elrith. This will show the world we are working to mend our issues and unite our peoples."

Well, when he put it like that, how could I refuse?

"Looks like we'll have another mouth to feed," Mason whispered to me. "She is a cute hellhound, much like her father was."

Dhun's smile slipped into a frown. "Kora is much cuter than I was."

Mason's smile turned into a serious expression as he nodded. "Of course she is."

My lips twitched as I fought a smirk against the outrage of Dhun's that we might think his daughter wasn't cuter than he'd been. He was a silly and proud dad and I loved that about him.

"Are you certain of this?" I asked once more.

Dhun immediately nodded. "Kora is very excited about her assignment and ability to learn from you all."

It would be nice for Elrith to have a friend at his side, someone who could protect him and support him at school where we wouldn't be able to go.

"We thank you for providing a guard for Elrith," I said and dipped my head.

Dhun stood and scowled at me. "Do not bow your head to me, Princess. I may be pack leader, but you far outrank me. Now, I will add that I plan to visit her once a month. Even though we can communicate mentally –"

"Nothing mental can change the comfort of physically being with a loved one and holding them in your arms," I said and smiled. "I also love knowing I'll get to see you frequently despite your new role. I feared you might be too busy for us now."

Dhun smiled softly and said, "I am always one summon away for you, Princess." One of the hellhounds yipped, drawing Dhun's attention. He nodded at them before turning back to us. "I must go, pressing matters to attend to, but I will be in contact soon." He pulled me into a hug and exhaled loudly. "I will see you soon."

I patted his back and said, "See you soon, friend."

He shifted into hellhound form, licked the side of Kora's face, and trotted away, his pack following him.

Kora whined softly once.

Elrith set a hand on her head between her ears and said, "It's okay, he'll be back to see you soon. Why don't we go play?"

Kora yipped and jumped around.

Elrith giggled and ran into the house, Kora on his heels.

"Not the first guard I'd thought to assign him, but reminds me of you," Trey said.

I looked up at him with a frown. "Of me?"

"Mason assigned himself as your guard when we were kids, so this is sort of like that," he replied and smiled down at me. "Elrith gets a hellhound while you had a raven."

"He's not wrong," Mason mumbled and wrapped his arms around my waist from behind, pressing a kiss to the side of my head. "And I'll be your guard until one of us dies."

"No one's dying," I snapped, and gripped one of the arms wrapped around me.

He rubbed his head against mine and said, "Easy, Lily."

Sighing, I rested my head against his shoulder. "Sorry."

Even though I knew I was safer here, my instincts were still on edge from all of the previous instances of trauma in the other world.

"Let's go inside and make sure the kids aren't destroying everything," Kayden said and pulled me away from Mason to tuck me beneath his arm as we walked inside. "We'll have to figure out what Kora likes to eat and—"

I'd been looking up at him, but when he stopped talking, mouth hung open as he stared ahead, I turned in that direction as well.

Elrith sat on the floor cross-legged, building something out of blocks and across from him sat an adorable little girl, about his age, with blonde hair that had blonde quills mixed among the strands.

"Looks like she gained powers from her father after he gained his new mantle," Trey commented.

"Guess we'll be registering two children into school here, not just one," Mason said and squatted down next to the two. "Hello, Kora. Can you tell us if there are certain foods you like and ones you don't like?"

"Meat! I like meat!" she shouted in a high-pitched voice with a huge smile on her face.

"What about what you don't like?" Mason asked again.

"Vegetables! No vegetables!"

"Veggies are important to help you grow strong," Elrith lectured.

She pouted. "Daddy didn't eat vegetables and none of the other hounds do. Why do I have to?"

"Those who can shift into these types of forms require vegetables for nutrition," Trey explained gently as he sat, cross-legged, between them. He picked up one of the blocks and added it to the tower Elrith had been working on. "Just like this block helps make the tower taller, the vegetables help make you taller."

Kora huffed, but said, "I'll try them, I guess."

"I'm going to go to the other world and get some food supplies. Is there anything specific you want?" Kayden asked.

"Cake!" Elrith shouted.

"Ice cream!" I shouted.

"Meat!" Kora shouted.

Kayden chuckled. "Cake, ice cream, and meat. Got it. I'll be back soon." He squeezed me and whispered in my ear, "I'll also update your parents about the newest addition."

"Ask Mom to order some outfits for Kora, please? She looks like she's probably in size eight kids' clothing."

He kissed the shell of my ear and whispered, "You got it."

"Don't forget we're going to the castle at lunchtime, so meet us there if you're not back in time," Trey called out to Kayden's retreating back.

Kayden raised his arm to let him know he'd heard before walking out the front door.

I sat in the highbacked chair and watched Mason, Trey, Kora, and Elrith playing together in the living room of the castle the demons had built for us and a sense of rightness and familiarity settled deep in my chest. Kora wasn't ours, but she definitely fit with the group of us. She was the first, born hellhound with the ability to shift forms, likely due to her father's unique powers. She was like a hybrid, a unique being like me. Suddenly, the familiarity triggered a memory and I realized that it was because I'd had a vision of this over a year ago. I'd thought it had been a simple dream due to Elrith's and Kora's appearances, of a being I'd never seen before, and I assumed it was my mind creating something.

Now, I understood the vision.

Trey and Mason looked at me, both with their heads slightly canted and a slight frown.

Was my shock filtering through the bond? It was going to take some getting used to and practice to keep from so openly sharing my emotions with them.

"Mama, come help us with the tower," Elrith said.

"Please, Princess!" Kora begged.

Both looked at me with wide, earnest, and eager eyes.

How could I say no to that?

"I'm not the best at building, but I'll help as much as I can," I promised as I slid off the chair, tucking my dress around my knees as I joined them in their circle.

Trey and Mason smiled at me, joy filtering through the bond from the both of them, and the warmth in my chest grew even more.

A found family. Exactly what I'd always wanted. Perfection.

CHAPTER
NINETEEN

Two weeks in the demon world and I felt as good as I had before I'd unlocked my other shadow powers.

Elrith and Kora were a full-time job, both so full of energy and the desire for knowledge that we'd hired private tutors, one from each world, since the demon world's school wasn't quite ready yet.

They were both being spoiled to an extreme level by my family, but I was okay with it. They deserved to be spoiled and shown what it was like to have a family like I was fortunate enough to find. Nana Jolie and Great Aunt Leona were the worst perpetrators, finding an excuse at least every other day to meet up to spend time with them.

Maya had been extra busy with courting my brother Tony, elf Tony, and Jaeden. Things were going well, though, and it helped ease my worry that I was neglecting our friendship. We did schedule a monthly girls' night with Piper, Maya, and I as well, swapping between worlds each month to keep our friendships stronger.

Azgon had volunteered to run the demon orphanage with the help of a few other females as staff. Jol had assured us she was a great choice because she was hard to rile up, making her perfect to handle children, and she was a strong fighter, so she could protect them as well. I still wanted to find and hire a few guards, which was on my to-do list when we returned.

Dad had called me back to Jinla to be part of a press conference to announce the identification process was going live for the demons and next week, visitations between worlds would be allowed.

I sat beside Mom, Jol on my other side, wearing a business suit with my hair tied back and light makeup on. My smile stayed in place as pictures and videos were being taken during the press conference.

Trey was at the dragons, dealing with some more drama from his cousins since Grandpa Rhys was here with us.

I looked down the line of my adoptive family at the table and my smile turned into a true one. It still astonished me that they had so easily accepted me being part demon and so quickly moved to unify us.

"We will take questions now," Grandpa Rhys announced.

Dozens of reporters' hands shot up into the air.

He chose one, but before the reporter could ask a question, a woman stood, anger contorting her face, and clapped her hands together.

A large fireball shot towards me, but I didn't even blink.

Grandpa Nico sighed, made a barrier, and the fireball sputtered out against it immediately.

Guards grabbed the woman, binding her, and escorted her from the room.

Five more people, three men and two women, stood, chanting as they began to attack.

Thankfully, most of the reporters present had been to press conferences with us before, so they knew to stay seated and let the guards and us handle things.

Mason, who had been leaning against the wall on the side of the room, drew his sword and leapt into action, taking down two of them while other guards took out the remaining three.

I arched a brow at him, but he ignored me.

"Seems like someone doesn't like you getting so much attention," Dad teased.

"I think he's just happy to get to fight something," I commented with a shrug.

Kayden tapped my bond, so I turned around to look at him where he stood against the back wall, holding Elrith, Kora at his side.

Elrith's eyes were glossy with unshed tears and he made a grabbing motion with one hand at me.

I nodded once to let Kayden know it was okay.

Kayden set Elrith on his feet and he immediately rushed onto the stage and to me.

I picked him up and set him on my lap, resting my chin atop his head, between his horns.

"Your mama is safe, promise," Mom cooed and stroked his back. "Her grandpas won't let anything happen to her."

I opened my mouth to reassure him when chains burst from the floor to wrap around my legs.

Dad leapt to his feet, snarling, and yelled, "Enough!"

The chains disappeared and a man in the crowd cried out in pain.

Lifting my eyes, I saw Mason standing behind a male mage, the tip of his sword dripping with blood poked out the front of the man's chest.

"These attacks will not be tolerated!" Grandpa Nico yelled, his voice and power making the room quake.

Elrith turned and growled at the audience, baring his fangs.

I stroked his hair and whispered, "It's alright, imp. The chains just startled me. No pain."

Dad had reacted so quickly that I'd only had time to notice them before they were gone.

"I knew there would be opposition, and you'd told me before that you've been attacked, but seeing this..." Jol paused and shook his head. "...it's no wonder you chose our world to live in."

"It's the life of a royal here," Mom said, a deep frown on her face. "People think that they can change things with our deaths, but all they do is forge our bonds stronger."

The attacks ceased and the kings answered a few questions. Once the time limit was up for questions, we made our way to the main hall. Jol, Elrith, and I would be the first demons to get ID cards.

Jol went first, taking a picture and waiting for the card to be printed.

Elrith went next, then me. The three of us stood together, holding our cards, and smiled for photos.

Once the reporters left, Kayden brought Kora over to get her ID as well.

Kora linked hands with Elrith and asked, "You okay?"

Elrith nodded. "Mad people tried to hurt Mama," he whispered.

Jol set his hand on Elrith's shoulder and said, "It's a good thing she has such a strong family and mates, right?"

Elrith nodded, but said, "Why do they hate her and us? Mama is nice."

Dad squatted down to look in Elrith and Kora's eyes and explained, "People are scared of things they do not understand and things that are different. It wasn't long ago that hybrids were the ones being attacked. It will take time, but eventually, they will see how great this change is and how great you are."

"They will?" Kor asked, hope in her eyes.

Dad nodded. "Yes, they will."

Well, many of them would. No matter what, there would always be people who hated others just because they were different.

"Come on, Grandma Ember and I are going to take you out for ice cream!" Dad announced.

Mom hugged me and said, "We'll see you at the house when you're ready to head back."

I squeezed her and nodded. "We're just packing up a few last items and getting our month's food supply."

"We need to stop at the clothing store to pick up Kora and Elrith's new wardrobes as well," Mason reminded me.

"New clothes?" Kora gasped.

I nodded, smiling down at her and said, "Including some dresses I saw you looking at."

She squealed and hugged me around the hips, the highest point she could reach. "Thank you, Princess!"

I tsked.

"Auntie," she quickly amended.

It felt too weird for her to call me by my title, so we had settled on me being her aunt.

"Have fun with your grandparents," I called as they, with Jol, walked towards the elevator to go to the garage where their vehicles waited.

"Are you ready, Princess?" Jeremy asked.

Since we were in Jinla, my family had forced guards on us, including the new mage, Jeremy, facing me now. After today's attacks, I was okay with the backup.

I nodded. "The car?"

"Out front," he confirmed. "Security has a path ready."

Mason set a hand on my lower back and said, "Deep breath. You're vibrating with nervous energy."

The nervousness wouldn't leave me, but I couldn't really explain it either. I obeyed, taking a deep breath and letting it out before we made our way out of the building and down the lane the security had made for us.

Reporters and people shouted at us, cameras flashed, blindingly, but we continued forward until we were inside the vehicle and secured.

Kayden directed Piper where to go and we moved off at a comfortable place.

"How does it feel to be one of the first demons with

access to this world?" Piper asked, glancing up in the rearview mirror with a smirk.

"Same as it did yesterday," I replied, and shrugged.

She laughed and shook her head. "I don't envy the amount of work that Trey's PR people are putting in on your social media accounts. People can be awful shitbags."

"That's an understatement," Mason grumbled.

"You can't kill everyone just because they don't like that your mate is a demon," Piper said.

"Watch me," Mason snapped.

I set a hand on his leg, and he exhaled harshly. "You okay?"

"I'm frustrated that I had to protect you today. You were giving a press conference with our son there and they still attacked you. They would have killed you without hesitation. Just because you're part demon. Even though you fucking saved all of us from becoming enslaved to that douchebag hybrid advisor."

"Saving the world doesn't give you an automatic pass," I said and shrugged.

"Just look at Jolie. She's been attacked a lot, as well as King Caleb. Shitty people are just going to be shitty," Piper said.

Still, something didn't feel right, but I couldn't put a finger on what it was to let anyone know.

Kayden sensed my unease and set a hand on my leg. "We're here. It's okay."

For now... I just felt like we were going to be attacked at any moment.

"We're going to go to the store first to pick up the items.

Are you sure you want to go in?" Piper asked. "You can wait in the car while one of us goes to get them instead."

"That might be better," I agreed with a nod, leaned my head back against the seat, and closed my eyes. "I can't stop feeling nervous or like we're about to engage in battle. I don't want to go into public any more than I have to right now."

"Understood," she said and nodded once.

I smiled at my friend and how professional she was being. Though, when it came to my safety, she was always top notch.

"Look," Kayden whispered and showed me pictures of Kora and Elrith eating a huge four scoop ice cream cone.

Their eyes were shining with such genuine joy that it made me smile and relax a bit. While I didn't like being away from them, I knew my mom and dad were the best protection they could have.

We parked in the garage of the mall and waited while they retrieved the kids' wardrobes. Once those were obtained, we resumed our drive towards home.

My body started to relax the closer to home we go. Clearly, it had all just been unnecessary worry on my part.

As we rounded the bend to enter our neighborhood, a loud beep sounded and the next thing I knew, we were engulfed in fire and airborne.

CHAPTER

TWENTY

Gasping in air, I tried to orient myself, but the only thing I could feel was pain and extremely hard ground pressing against my body.

My ears rang so loudly and dizziness made my vision swim, so I couldn't figure out which way was up.

Someone touched me, but it caused extreme pain to flare through my body and I cried out in pain, pushing at the hands, trying to ward them off.

My eyes slowly blinked open and the first thing I saw was blood on the back of Kayden's head that lay on the pavement before me. "Kay?" I croaked and tried to reach out towards him, but my body wouldn't move.

"Stay still, Lily," Piper ordered me. "A healer is on the way."

The ringing had subsided and what was left was almost worse as a torrent of sounds assaulted me.

"There was a bomb on our vehicle, human made, which

is why we didn't detect it with magic," she explained as she knelt next to me.

"De-Dead?" I gasped.

"No, no one died, but all of us are injured. We seem to be safe, but—"

Her words were cut off by the roar of a dragon.

Sadly, not the one I was mated to.

I tugged on Trey's bond, jerking it as hard as I could with my limited powers at the moment.

Piper stood on wobbly legs, one of her arms hanging limply by her side, and took a warrior shift with a sword in the hand that seemed to be working. "Protect the royals!" she shouted.

Jeremy limped over as quickly as he could and put up a barrier just in time to protect us from the first dragon's breath aimed at us. He dropped to one knee, sucking in sharp gasps as he gripped his staff and held the barrier in place.

Where was Mason? I could feel the bond, but not where he was. Was he unconscious? I knew he wasn't dead, because I would have felt that pain, but I was too weak to do anything else.

Closing my eyes, I tried to mentally communicate with my fathers, trying to get someone nearby who could help us. Or someone who could get Dad or Mom to teleport to us and help fight.

The disorientation I was dealing with made it hard to even do that, so I wasn't sure if anyone heard me.

"Give us Liliana and we'll let the rest of you live," a familiar male voice said.

Who was that? I knew the voice, but ... who?

"What is the meaning of this, Alexander? Do you think you won't be punished for this?" Piper asked.

"Doesn't matter as long as I take her out," he grunted.

My mate's cousin was attacking me. Wow.

"Spineless. Piece. Of. Shit," I gasped out as I pushed up onto my hands and knees.

He growled. "What?"

I turned my head slowly to look at him. "Couldn't. Handle us. Full power. Used humans. Pathetic. Dragon. Bastard."

He roared and tried to use a fire breath, but Jeremy's shield was still intact.

I gripped the back of Piper's shirt as I stood and we leaned against each other, helping to stay upright. "Going to. Watch Trey. Gut you. Put your head. On mantle," I gasped out. I definitely had ribs broken. No doubt about it. Thankfully, we had decently fast healing rates, so as long as we could hold out, we could heal and fight them.

He spat to the side. "He'll thank me for curing him of your stench."

The vehicle we'd been in was completely destroyed and burning about fifty feet from us. Had we flown out of it and landed on the pavement here? There was broken glass everywhere, which made it hard to find a safe spot to rest.

Piper had blood dripping down her limp arm and there was a dark patch on her back that concerned me, but there wasn't time to check injuries and assess our condition.

"I'm going to pull your spine from your body and use it as a coatrack," Kayden snarled as he stood up behind us. Blood dripped down his face and onto his shoulder, but his eyes glowed with unbridled fury and he otherwise looked unharmed.

"We do need. New coat rack... in... the house," I said with a smile at him.

Kayden didn't look at me as he shifted into his warrior form and ran out of the shield, straight at Alexander.

A dizzy spell hit me and I fell to my knees, but I kept my eyes glued to the fight, needing to watch my mate fighting our enemy.

Piper growled. "Reinforcements are on the way. We just have to hold out until they arrive."

Turning my head, I found Mason about four feet from us, unconscious on the ground. I hissed in pain as I forced my body to walk over to him. "Mas?" I whispered and slid to my knees next to him, resting a hand on his back. He was breathing, but there was a puddle of blood near his head that worried me.

Trey tugged on the bond and I tugged harder as Kayden took a hard hit to the face from Alexander. I knew Trey and I should be able to communicate mentally, but the four of us hadn't figured it quite out yet.

A wolf howled and my hair stood on end as I turned to look behind us. Three werewolves in warrior form approached, snarling and prepared to fight.

"If you do this, your life is forfeit," Piper yelled out to them. "King Deryn and Dan will not forgive you harming Lily. You know this. Why are you being stupid?"

"Once we end her life, they'll see the demons for the true threat that they are. She's covering for them, putting them in a positive light. We know. We've been attacked and had family killed by them," one of the wolves said.

Ah, it made sense now. These were people who had experienced loss at the hands of the demons and couldn't let it go. Couldn't accept that things that had happened before our truce could be forgiven. That there were bad apples in every group.

"I... didn't do anything," I challenged. "I've always... supported the wolves and other races."

If Mason would just wake up, be safe, he could protect us. He was our best fighter.

Reaching into my pocket, I pulled out my phone, but the device was completely destroyed. Useless.

"Mine's broken, too," Piper whispered and gripped her sword harder.

"I can't hold a shield... much... longer," Jeremy gasped.

People had started to come out of their houses, but when they saw there was a battle about to happen, they went back inside. At least they had seen us, perhaps they would call to get us help.

"Hurry, before they get help," one of the wolves snarled and charged at us.

Protect. I had to protect Mason. Had to help keep Piper and the others safe, too. It wasn't their fault they were assigned to us. They didn't deserve to die because of who I was.

Reaching deep within myself, I drew on my power and coaxed what I could out to take a partial warrior shift, scales flowing over my vital parts as the werewolves breached the shield. I also made sure that my shift included a partial tail.

The first werewolf reached me and I punched him as hard as I could in the chest, sending him backwards, away from Mason's prone form. I seemed to be their target, but I couldn't let them get Mason while he was vulnerable. Risking them getting Mason to hurt me wasn't an option.

The werewolf swiped his claws down my arm, slicing through skin down to the bone and causing me to cry out in pain.

I kicked him away, clutching my arm, which bled profusely.

"We can make this easy, Princess. Let us put you out of your misery," he said as he circled me.

"I am Princess Liliana of the Hybrids and Demons. I will purge your hatred from the clans. I will go down fighting you to protect others you may target next."

"You can't even protect yourself," he scoffed and kicked me in the chest.

My broken ribs that had just started repairing themselves cracked again from the kick and worse from hitting the ground.

The air whooshed from my lungs and I couldn't breathe. Black tendrils clouded my vision.

More dragons roared, but I had no idea if they were friend or foe.

Was this it? Was this how I died?

Getting to my feet, I barely stood upright before he tried to slice his claws across my face. Spinning around, I hit him with my tail, sending him flying into one of his accomplices that had been fighting Piper, saving her from his attack.

"Get Mason and get out of here," I ordered her.

She gritted her teeth and shook her head. "Not leaving you."

"I am ordering you!" I shouted.

"No!" she shouted back, turning to face the werewolves as they returned to fight us.

"Stubborn bitch," I hissed at her.

"Takes one to know one," she snapped back.

Two dragons dropped out of the sky and my jaw dropped as Trey's mother was one of them. She was in a warrior shift, something I didn't realize she was capable of.

"You," I hissed. "You orchestrated this?"

She bared her teeth at me. "It wasn't hard to find others who want you dead as much as I do. So, why don't you just accept your fate and die so that Trey can move on and find someone worthy of him."

"Your son won't even grieve for you and no funeral will be held as I'm going to burn your body and let your ashes wash down the sewer pipes!" I bellowed and ran at her.

A breath of fire whooshed out of her, but I dodged to the side and continued my approach.

Luckily for me, she wasn't a trained fighter and despite my injuries, it wasn't long before I had her wrapped up in my coils. I hesitated for a second, debating whether I should crush her or not. While she was evil and would have killed me had she had the ability, she was still Trey's mother. Would he hate me for killing her even though I was protecting myself?

My hesitation gave one of the werewolves a chance to run over and attack me, their claws cutting into my scales and skin.

I screamed, but instead of loosening, I tightened my hold more. Bones cracked and after a second, her heart stopped beating against my underbelly.

Shifting quickly, I rolled away from her body and faced the werewolf who continued to advance on me.

He drew a sword from his back and smiled evilly. "This ends now, Princess."

From the corner of my eye, I saw reinforcements arrive in the form of two of my adoptive fathers, Branson and Riddick.

Relief surged through me, but it was short lived as I had to duck and dodge away from the werewolf's sword.

I stumbled over a piece of the car smoldering on the ground and the werewolf thrust his sword towards me.

Branson was suddenly there, between the werewolf and me, taking the sword to his stomach in my place.

"Bran!" I screamed.

He elbowed the werewolf behind him, forcing him to release his hold on the sword and jerked it out himself with a grunt.

I scrambled to my feet, gripping his shirt to pull it up to check, but he grabbed me in a bone-crunching hug. "We're here, Lily. We've got you."

"Bran Bran," I sobbed.

He suddenly released me, spinning around and took a warrior shift, his body becoming mostly bear, and roared at the attacking werewolves and dragons. His roar shook the windows on the nearby houses and for a split second, fear crossed the faces of the werewolves near us.

Riddick knelt by Mason, checking him over.

"Go sit with Mason while we handle this," Branson ordered me.

"Yes, Dad," I whispered as I limped over to my still unconscious mate.

The werewolf who had stabbed him tried to run around Branson at me, but Branson grabbed him around the throat and lifted him off the ground, strangling him. "You hurt my daughter, so now you die."

The werewolf's screams followed me as I limped towards Mason and a smile spread over my face knowing Bran Bran was killing the one who had hurt me and my mates.

Riddick had gone off to help Piper with the dragon and wolf she was fighting against, so it was just Mason and I as I sat down on the pavement, being careful not to sit on broken glass.

Kayden was still fighting Alexander, seemingly in a stalemate as both sucked in breaths and bled from various injuries, about ten feet apart, glaring and snarling at each other.

Mason's body suddenly jerked and he went from laying on the ground to standing in the blink of an eye. Black shadows danced across his skin a moment before disappearing. He looked down at me, an expression I hadn't seen before on his handsome face, his eyes black orbs that glowed with power. "Lily, safe?" he asked in a deeper than usual voice.

I nodded. "I'm safe."

He turned and took in the scene before us. With an eerie growl and chirp, he sprinted across the road towards Kayden and Alexander.

What was that? I had never seen him act that way before or have black eyes? Was it from the piece of my power that he had inside of him?

Too many questions without a simple or known answer.

A new dragon roared and this time, I relaxed, recognizing the roar of my mate, Trey.

"Took you long enough," I whispered just before my body fell to the side and I slipped into unconsciousness.

CHAPTER
TWENTY-ONE

"Mama?" I whispered as I felt her running her hands along my body and using her magic to heal me.

"It's alright, baby. We're here and you and your mates are safe now," she whispered back, her voice thick with emotion.

"Piper? The other guards?" I asked.

"All safe. Nana Kara is healing Piper right now," she assured me.

I exhaled in relief. "Trey mad?" I asked, my voice cracking as I feared his reaction to finding out I had killed his mother.

"No, Lily, he's not mad at you," she assured me.

"Elrith and Kora?" I asked.

"Safe with Triston and Jol at the house," she answered. "We'd just arrived at the house when Branson felt your call for help and notified us." She sniffled. "It took us a little longer to find out where you were, but luckily he and Riddick were closest."

"Stop talking," Great Nana Kara snapped at us. "You're impending Ember's healing ability and you've got a lot to heal. All of you do."

"I do?"

She scoffed. "Seven broken ribs, severe lacerations, some down to the bone, burns across a lot of your body, and more."

"Burns from explosion?" I guessed.

"Child, shush," she said in exasperation.

I obeyed, but cracked open one eye to look up at Mom. Both eyes opened at the sight of her glowing eyes brimming with tears. "Mama?"

"I crushed them, Lily. I used my powers and crushed the rest of them into dust," she said. "And I'd do it again in a heartbeat."

Mom could use telekinesis and had an affinity for earth, which meant she could pull rock from the ground and use it to crush people.

"It's not enough," she snarled. "They should have been punished, not killed, but I couldn't stop myself when I saw you bleeding on the ground." Leaning down, she nuzzled my cheek with her nose. "I'm so sorry this happened to you."

"Not your fault," I reminded her.

"We should have found you another family to live in, one that wasn't so dangerous to be part of. If you'd been raised by another, non-royal family, then you wouldn't have been forced to live like this. You would have been safe."

I shook my head and reached up to grip one of her hands. "What do you think would have happened if I'd ended up in a family who despised demons? Do you think they would have reacted so rationally to finding out I was part demon? That I was a demon princess? No, I was raised in the right family and it's thanks to your training and parenting that none of us died today."

"Lily!" Trey yelled and ran over to kneel beside us. He rested a hand on my cheek and rubbed his thumb across my cheekbone. "Stop talking and let your mom heal you."

"I'm sorry," I whispered. "I'm so sorry, Trey. If there had been another way."

He growled at me and I snapped my mouth shut, pain shooting through me at the anger on his face.

Mom growled at him.

"I'm the one who's sorry. I knew they were up to something, that they were planning something, but I ignored it, focused on their trivial bullshit instead of seeing what I should have. I should have known that my mother would try to hurt you, especially after my father and she separated."

"You're not mad at me?"

His face softened and he leaned down to press a gentle kiss against my forehead. "My beautiful, stubborn mate, I am a lot of things right now, but mad at you for protecting yourself is not one of them. I wish I had shown up sooner to save you from so much pain."

"Kay and Mas?" I asked.

"We're safe, love," Mason answered from somewhere behind me.

"I'm trying to heal you lot!" Great Nana Kara snapped. "Stop talking and let us heal you."

"Yes, Nana," all of us replied simultaneously.

Once they finished healing us, we were forced to let Dad teleport us to the house where Mason, Kayden, and I were ordered to lay on the couches while we waited for them to finish things up there.

Elrith ran to me, Kora in her hellhound form at his side, and they climbed onto the couch with me, cuddling with me silently.

"We're all safe and sound," I reassured them as I pet both of their heads.

Triston rested a hand atop my hair and whispered, "I'm glad they made it in time."

"Thanks, Dad," I whispered back, my eyes heavy. "I think I'm going to take a nap."

"You do that, child. Jol, Trey, and I will keep you safe," he promised.

Though Mom had healed me, I was still depleted of energy and magic. A nap would help with that, but I really needed to return to the demon world to recuperate. Again.

"Trey, with me!" Triston suddenly snapped.

I opened my eyes and watched as Trey and Triston ran out of the house.

"Perimeter breach," I whispered to Kayden and Mason, getting to my feet, Elrith in my arms.

Kora stood on the ground in her hellhound form, her quills puffed out and rattling as she growled at the door.

Out there, I could sense several powerful beings, but I had no idea if they were friend of foe.

"Stay here," Mason ordered Kayden and us.

He opened the door and was immediately blown backwards by a huge fireball to the chest. His body slammed into the living room wall and I screamed his name.

Kayden ran in front of us, shielding the three of us with his body.

The sounds of fighting and Jol's roar drew me towards the door and I blinked in shock as I stared at a group of over a dozen beings, a mixture of werewolves, dragon shifters, and mages, fighting Triston, Trey, and Jol.

Why? Why was this happening to us?

I don't know where the knowledge suddenly came from, but I knew exactly what I needed to do. The plan and knowledge of how to execute it was just … within me.

I stepped forward to exit the front door, but Kayden called my name stopping me. I turned and thrust Elrith into his arms.

When I turned back around, I felt the shadows dancing along my skin just before they spread out to touch the shadows of everyone in the front yard fighting, freezing them all in place.

My lips twitched as I fought a smile, overjoyed that some of my shadow powers had returned at last.

"Lily, what's your plan?" Mason asked as he joined me at the door, his shirt gone, the burned scraps on the ground and a few bubbled blisters from the fire on his chest.

"I'm going to call for reinforcements," I said and smiled evilly. "They want to fight the Demon Princess? Well, then they're going to fight the Demon Princess."

Stepping out onto the grassy yard in front of the house, I spread my arms and closed my eyes, when I opened them again, I felt the portals behind me.

"Did you create the portals?" Mason asked softly.

I nodded.

"Your fight is not with Triston or the hybrids!" I shouted loud enough that everyone focused on me, eyes the only things they could move.

Trey's eyes focused on mine while the others stared with wide eyes at the three portals behind me, one of the portals taller than my parents' two-story house.

"Kora, a howl, please?" I requested.

Kora tilted her little snout up and released the most adorable howl I had ever heard.

Seconds later, Dhun and four other hellhounds stepped out of the left portal and came to sit behind me.

"Zoman. Huk. Tier'na," I summoned.

Zoman came through first wearing full armor, a sword in hand, and dropped to one knee beside me. "Princess?"

"Protect the king," I ordered him.

He dipped his head. "It shall be done." He walked over to Jol and bowed to him before taking a step forward, putting himself between Jol and the intruders.

I had to release the shadows freezing them as I was still too weak to hold it, but thankfully the enemies didn't immediately start attacking, their fear and confusion rooting them in place.

"What is this?" one of the mages asked.

"You trespassed on hybrid lands, intent on killing demons, while I, Princess of Hybrids *and* Demons, am here. Did you think I wouldn't protect my family? Did you think you could do as you liked, unchecked, on lands I protect? Unlike you uppity, separatists, demons protect each other, especially our royalty. Your intentions to kill King Jol and I are clear, and the fact that you'd also willingly kill my adopted son is an even larger mark against you."

From the center portal, the one taller than the house, a giant werewolf-like demon stepped through, much like the one that had fought us in the park. This one normally wandered around the far mountains, away from the castle, but I'd watched him often.

"Huk," I greeted, and he dipped his head to me before growling at the gathered enemies. Shadows danced amongst his black fur, making it look like fire.

From the right portal, a female from Talrnir's village, Tier'na, exited and made her way to stand before Kayden, Elrith, and Kora. She carried twin blades that sparked with lightning and wore leather armor, her hair braided down the sides of her head, and an angry snarl on her face, showing off serrated teeth in her mouth.

"Tier'na, protect the children and my mate as you take them home," I ordered her.

"It shall be done," she said.

"Get them through the portal and home," I ordered Kayden.

"No, Lily!" he yelled. "I'm not leaving you."

Turning, I met his eyes and said, "That's an order, Kayden."

His back went rigid, body turned stiffly, robotically, and with Kora and Tier'na at his heels, they ran for the nearest portal.

I closed that portal and faced our enemies again. "I am Liliana Rubyserpent, Daughter of Queen Ember and King

Caleb of the Hybrids, Descendent of Third to Reign, Princess of Hybrids and Demons. You have declared war on my clans, attacked my mate and king, and your lives are now forfeit. Kill them and let none escape."

Dhun howled, Huk roared, and everyone charged forward.

"Fuck, you're absolutely stunning," Mason said as he pulled me into his chest and kissed me deeply. "A fucking goddess."

"Now is not the time for making out," I said and pushed him back, a smile on my face.

"Later, I'm going to worship your body like the goddess you are deserves," he promised as he drew his sword.

A mage teleported next to me and Mason managed to cut through the mage's staff and chest before he could cast his next spell.

Triston ran to me. "You shouldn't be using so much magic when you're not recuperated. The others are on their way."

"I'm not using magic anymore," I explained. "Being able to summon them by calling them is part of being a demon royal by blood. I only used magic to freeze everyone."

Mom and Dad teleported next to us, took in the scene, and Dad immediately charged into the fight with an eerie howl.

"Are you injured?" Mom asked as she ran her hands over me, inspecting me.

"I'm safe, Mom. Mason has some burns, but I think they're healing already."

"I'm fine," he said as he cut down a werewolf trying to get past him to me.

"To think they would breach our borders to attack you," Mom said with a sigh. "The sheer stupidity and audacity shouldn't surprise me, but it does. You should have called us right away."

"This was my fight, not yours," I countered.

"Every fight of yours is also mine," she argued back. "Plus, these are my lands that they trespassed on."

A mage teleported next to us, a fireball in his hand, but Mom opened a portal beneath his feet, making him fall through it and right in front of Huk who slapped the mage with his giant hand, a hand the size of the mage, and sent him flying into a tree. The mage's body made a sickening crack against the tree and his limp body fell to the ground.

"All of this death was unnecessary," I shouted to those fighting. "Your deaths serve no purpose except to make us sad that you're so blinded by hate that you were willing to give your lives for it."

"We won't stop until you're all dead!" a female dragon yelled as she fought against Trey, both in dragon warrior forms.

"Capture her," Mom ordered Branson in a sharp bark that startled me.

Branson and Riddick worked with Trey to subdue the female dragon enough to drag her towards the cells.

"Why capture her?" I asked Mom.

"I think they have a group, an organization of sorts, that's been created to fight the demons. We're going to question her and find out who is behind it all," she explained.

"Like there used to be for those that hated the hybrids?" I asked, remembering how they'd told me about having to deal with extreme hatred and attacks as well when she was being courted by my fathers.

She nodded, a scowl on her face. "For all we know, it could be some of the previous members, recreating what we'd thought destroyed. Hatred has been around us as long as I can remember."

It didn't take long for the rest of the enemies to be dispatched.

Trey walked to me, a fierce glow in his eyes, slid his hand around the back of my neck, and pulled me into a deep kiss. When he pulled back, I was dizzy for a second. "I think I just fell even more in love with you, my goddess."

Mom snickered behind her hand as she walked to Mason to finish the healing of his burns.

"Think Kayden will forgive me for sending him away?" I asked softly and rested my head against his chest as we sat on the porch steps.

He nodded, his chin rubbing the top of my head. "You needed at least one of us to go with the kids to ensure they're protected. He'll likely pout about not being able to fight, but logically know it was necessary."

"Should we take some of his favorite ice cream home as an apology gift?" I asked.

Trey chuckled and pushed me back. "You sure you just don't want some ice cream?"

"I do think I've earned it," I said and turned away so he wouldn't see my smirk.

"Your food order is in the outside fridge and freezer," Mom said from where she stood, healing Mason still. "You should get a cart to carry all the bags."

"I will carry," Huk said in a booming voice.

I smiled up at the giant demon. "That would be most appreciated, Huk."

A thought came to me and I asked, "Would you like a job, Huk?"

He tilted his head. "Job?"

"The children," I began explaining, "the ones whose parents are dead ..."

"Orphans?" he clarified.

I nodded and felt bad that I'd thought he might not know what that word was, that he might not be intelligent just because of how large he was. How could I fall to such a stereotype?

"The orphanage that was recently built, where the children will be, Azgon is the leader there, but I still worry for their safety. Would you be willing to work there, as their guard?"

"Protect demon orphans?" he asked.

I nodded. "Exactly."

He bowed. "It would be a great honor to protect the orphans at Princess Liliana's orphanage."

That solved one of my issues nicely!

"Thank you, Huk."

"Do you know of others who might be willing to be guards, who would never harm the children even if the children are injured?" Jol asked Huk.

Huk tilted his head up and thought for a moment. "I know two, strong fighters, never harm others unless attacked first. They are smart enough to understand the children will be the ones to protect and know not to harm them, even if the children act out against us."

"Please have them come see the princess to discuss working at the orphanage as well," Jol ordered.

Huk dipped his head in a bow. "As you wish, Your Majesty."

"Are you injured?" I asked Jol.

He shook his head. "You summoning Zoman prevented me from being able to fight."

I smiled at the indignation in his tone. "I apologize, but they were clearly intent on harming you. You wouldn't want to return to a certain female demon with wounds, would you?"

He folded his arms across his chest and said, "She would tend to me and praise me for my valiant deeds."

Mom laughed once before turning it into a cough. "Why are kings so similar no matter the race?"

Dad scowled at her as he walked to us, finished cleaning up the bodies. "What was that, mate?"

She smiled sweetly at him and batted her eyelashes. "I was asking if you'd like to go on a date, just the two of us, soon?"

He clearly knew she'd changed the question, but he smiled, slid an arm around her waist, and pulled her close to whisper something that made her giggle.

"Ew," I said and waved at them like that would make the mental image disappear.

Tony and Maya ran from the direction of town towards us, panting. "What ... What happened?" Tony gasped.

"A little late, bro," Mason teased.

"I didn't know something was wrong until a moment ago," he said, ears red.

"Were you two ... preoccupied?" I guessed.

Maya's pale face turned as red as her hair and she shouted, "Lily!"

Everyone laughed and I felt myself relax finally.

TWENTY-TWO

One of the attackers had streamed the fight somehow, and it spread like wildfire across the internet and social media.

The response to the videos was varied. Some supported me protecting my family and acknowledging that of course I would fight attackers who trespassed on hybrid lands. Others claimed that the powers I showed proved that I was a threat and should be dealt with. Those comments didn't stay up long, and I was fairly certain the team that Trey had hired to watch over social media about me were the ones handling those. There had also been a few death threats and those people were arrested quickly and quietly. Threats would not be tolerated.

There was one person making many comments supporting me and telling them that I was no more dangerous now than I was a year ago, it was just that my powers were now common knowledge. Whoever that person was, I was glad that they were on my side and so supportive. It showed that I did have friends out there, even if I also had haters. I kept those supporters in my mind whenever I read or heard something bad.

My fathers were able to get answers from the dragon woman they had captured, confirming Mom's suspicions that the former members of the group who had been after hybrids was now reformed and their focus was changed to going after demons instead.

An immediate notice went out from the Council announcing the hunt for those that were part of the organization and anyone who was caught as part of it would be punished swiftly. The fact that it came from the Council, and not just my parents, showing we were all unified, even the sirens, helped our cause a lot.

Within two weeks of the notice, a dozen members were outed by the community, but we still didn't know who was leading it, what they were planning, or where their base of operations was located.

The Council had put together a task force to find this new organization and the portal between our worlds was being heavily guarded and visitors thoroughly vetted before being allowed through.

In the demon world, things were progressing nicely. Since they didn't have social media or internet yet, they weren't aware of all of the negativity and the threats. Trade between worlds had opened a lot of doors, though, and we were well underway building the infrastructure necessary for electricity.

I sat in the gardens of Jol's castle, singing to the plants there were thriving in the newly fertilized soil. Kora and Elrith lay in my eyesight, napping in the midday sun. Mason was perched atop a scarecrow, one Elrith had built, his beak tucked beneath his wing as, he too, took a nap.

It was a peaceful day, the type that I hoped continued happening.

Trey lowered into a squat beside me, gently raising the leaf of the tomatoes I sat before. "They're really perking up since you started coming here and singing to them."

Smiling, I said, "I told you, talking and singing helps plants grow. It's been proven time and time again."

He sat, cross-legged, next to me and rested his head against my shoulder. "I'm going to rest while you keep singing."

Patting my thigh, I said, "Put your head on my lap. I'll pet your hair while I sing."

His eyes flashed, and I felt his lust through our bond, but he quickly tamped it down, and, despite being in a nice pair of slacks and an expensive, crème, button-up shirt, he lay on the dirt with his head on my thigh a second later.

I resumed singing, a song that Great Nana Kara had taught me when I would stay with them. It was meant as a healing song, one you sang while healing, to help with focus, but it seemed like a good song for the current situation.

Zoman wandered out of the castle, gave me a nod, sat on one of the stone benches that Grandpa Rhys had added to the garden, and leaned his back against the wall of the garden, his eyes closed.

One of the demon generals, Ta'Kur, a seven-foot-tall male with deep red horns that arched over the top of his head and curled up and out behind his head, wearing a leather outfit, walked out next, sat beside the children on the ground, and closed his eyes.

What was happening? Why were they all coming out here? Was my singing ... decent? Did they enjoy hearing me sing? Or was this just them placating me as a princess?

I switched songs, singing one I wasn't sure where I'd heard before, but was pretty sure it was something my biological father had sung when I was little. It was a hauntingly beautiful song that always made me smile when I sang it, though, I couldn't remember when I *had* last sung it.

Another demon general, Mita, the shortest general at four foot eleven, with huge biceps and curving horns like a goat, walked out next. He scowled at me, but dipped his head in greeting, sat in the far back corner, farthest from all of us, and wrapped his arms around his legs as he closed his eyes. He didn't hate me, but it was obvious he wasn't fully accepting of me just yet. Soon. Perhaps soon he would fully accept me. Still, it made me question even more, why was he out here?

I wasn't a siren, Dad had confirmed that, so what was going on?

Switching to a different song, I moved on to one from a famous band that toured all around the other world. It was upbeat and definitely out of my vocal range and yet ... everyone stayed still and content.

Perhaps it was best not to question it and just to continue.

Over the next hour, I switched between healing songs, ones Mom had sung to me, pop songs, and others I remembered. And over that hour, more demons joined us in the gardens and all of them, within minutes of joining us, fell asleep.

Jol walked out another hour later and smiled at me. "Your voice is very calming, especially in our original tongue. How did you learn it?"

I blinked up at him. "Wh-What? I'm not singing in a demon language. I'm singing in my native language."

He frowned down at me and shook his head. "No, that was definitely the demon language I heard coming out of your mouth just now."

"How could I know it if I had never been taught it and don't know it now?" I asked.

"Maybe it's something you learned young and forgot because your parents were trying to hide you?" Trey suggested as he sat up and rubbed his eyes. "It definitely felt like you put me under a spell, a good one, but still. It reminded me of the spells Jolie does sometimes with her siren abilities, it at least had that same feeling."

My brows rose into my hairline and I quickly got to my feet. "Where's Talrinir?" I demanded from Jol.

His eyes widened at my concerned tone, and he simply pointed at the castle.

Without waiting for words, I ran into the castle and up the stairs to the office that Talrinir had claimed for herself as the King's Advisor.

We all knew within a few months she would be the queen, but we let it slide without comment.

"Talrinir!" I yelled as I ran up the steps and turned the corner to her office.

She stood outside of it, a smile on her face as I ran up to her. "Done singing already? I quite enjoyed it."

"How do I know demonic?" I demanded.

She laughed and set her hand on my shoulder. "Come inside, friend. Let's have some tea while we chat."

I followed her into the office, taking in the additional bookshelves that I knew Jol had built specifically for her. There were several new books from the other world, some nonfiction about business and other boring topics, and some fiction ones that caught my eye, specifically romance novels.

"When did you start reading these?" I asked as I picked up the first book, showing her the cover with a shirtless man showing off his abs.

She shrugged. "They have good storylines most times. Though, there are a couple I gave up on partway through. I'll try them at a later date."

I returned her shrug. "Some books aren't for everyone. I remember a really popular series that was going around at my high school and I tried to read it, but hated the main character."

"Sit and I'll get the tea," she said and waved at the couch and coffee table on the far side of the room.

The questions that were still unanswered bottled up in my throat, but I knew Talrinir and she would make me wait until she was ready to talk. So, I sat on the couch and waited while she prepared tea for us.

When she set the tea down, she also set down a few cucumber sandwiches and I quickly stuffed two in my mouth. My eyes widened, and she laughed.

"I could hear your stomach grumbling from the door when you ran up here," she told me. "I'm surprised you didn't notice it."

"My surprise at knowing a language I wasn't taught

trumped my hunger, apparently," I said around the food, hiding my mouth behind my hand.

"About that," she said and took a sip of her tea before continuing. "Your parents taught you when you were little. I'm surprised you remember it, but I have heard you use some demonic words before. I thought you'd picked them up while you'd been stuck here, but it makes sense that a language you were taught when you were little would stay with you. Especially as a royal. Also, there are strange magical connections that we have as demons and many kids barely have to be taught the language, to later just intuitively knowing it." She shrugged. "I don't really have a proper explanation except ..." She made wiggling motions with her fingers, smiled wide, and said in a silly, wobbly voice, "... magic."

"Really? Magic? That's it?" I gaped at her.

Sipping more tea, she nodded. "Sorry, friend, that's all I have. We don't teach the kids in our villages demonic and yet they'll use it sometimes. I think, perhaps, we were taught it and the Grand Advisor used his spells to teach us your language instead, but ..." She shrugged. "That doesn't always add up completely. Honestly, why worry about it? It's not like it's a bad thing for you to know the language."

"Why did my singing feel like a spell to them? I'm not part siren, Dad would have known if I were."

She smiled and set her cup down. "Oh, that one is easy! As a royal, you have the ability to change our people's emotions with your voice. It was an ability only blood royals were able to use. Jol can't use it, sadly, but you clearly can. I almost fell asleep while you were singing, so I had to close my window."

"So, it's like a siren's ability to alter emotions," I whispered to myself as I picked up another sandwich.

"I'm not familiar with your sirens, but yes."

"I feel like I'm always learning new things about myself, finding new abilities."

"You mean like your ability to summon specific demons and open a portal for them?" she guessed.

"Exactly," I nodded.

"Well, with some of your abilities gone, it makes sense that you would uncover other abilities. Your unconscious self needs to find ways to protect yourself."

"Isn't that what we are for?" Mason asked from the window.

Talrinir gasped and cursed at him. "Mason!"

He smirked and sat on the windowsill. "Sorry, Talrinir."

"You get used to him popping up in windows randomly," I muttered.

"I don't think I ever will," she said and exhaled harshly. "Just use the door like a normal person."

"I flew up here," he explained as he sat beside me, draped an arm around my shoulders, and plucked the sandwich from my fingers to pop it into his mouth and eat it.

"Your mate needs food," Talrinir instructed as she picked her cup back up. "My snacks aren't enough for all that growling going on."

"That's not you growling at me?" Mason asked her, blinked down at me with wide eyes, and picked me up in a bridal carry. "Why didn't you tell us you are hungry?"

"She didn't realize it in her urgency to find out why she could speak demonic," Talrinir explained. Flipping one of her ears over her shoulder, she added, "I don't growl at others."

"You growled at me yesterday," I reminded her.

Scowling she said, "You were being obstinate."

Mason laughed and headed towards the door.

I waved at Talrinir over his shoulder. "I'll come see you tomorrow for the next education meeting. Noon?"

"Yes, noon," she agreed with a nod. "Druth said to drop the children off after breakfast with her as she has something important to teach them."

"What is it?"

She shrugged. "Your guess is as good as mine. Go eat." She waved at me dismissively just as Mason stepped out of her office and the door closed behind us.

Wrapping my arms around his neck, I snuggled close, resting my forehead against his cheek. "You smell good."

"As do you," he replied. "But she is right, your stomach is growling a lot. Let's collect the kids and Trey so we can go home and get food. I'm hungry as well."

"Food?" Kora shouted from the castle entrance.

"Yes, we're going home to get food," Mason answered.

She yipped and the quills in her hair vibrated in her excitement. "Trey! Elrith! We're going home! Food!"

"Food!" Elrith shouted.

Mason chuckled. "Seems you aren't the only hungry one amongst us. We'll have to make a lot if both the kids are that hungry."

"Kayden's already started prepping food," Trey advised as he joined us at the castle's entrance. Half of his shirt and pants, the side he'd been lying on, was brown from the dirt now.

"I hope it's tasty," I said and licked my lips.

Trey wiped something from my chin and said, "I'm certain he's doing his best to make you and the imps tasty food."

"Come on, let's race home!" Mason said, and immediately took off at a sprint.

"Cheater!" Elrith yelled after us, but very quickly caught up, his wings flapping to give him extra push as he ran.

TWENTY-THREE

Trey guided me away from our house in the demon world, hands on my shoulders, a blindfold over my eyes. "Almost there," he promised.

"It feels like it's been an hour, so I hope so," I muttered, grumpy because I wanted to know what this surprise was.

Elrith giggled next to me. "Mama doesn't like surprises."

"No, she does not," Kayden agreed with him. "That's why we try to give her one at least every few months. Keeps things interesting."

I growled at him, which earned me laughs from everyone.

We'd walked through a mostly silent area, then through a noisy area full of voices and sounds that I assumed was the city, then to a quiet area again. Were we on the opposite side of the city? I tried to mentally picture the area and the side I thought we were on was just a field.

Trey stopped me and removed the blindfold.

After my eyes adjusted to the bright sun, my hands flew to my mouth as I gasped and tears sprang to my eyes. We stood atop a small hill that allowed us to look over the field below. Only, there wasn't a field anymore. Over a dozen houses had been built, creating a little suburban area, and there were already demons living in the houses, tending to their yards, which I noticed had not grass and flowers, but crops behind each one.

The reason for the tears was the excitement that my people were getting better housing and that my grandparents and parents had helped with this in secret, but also because every door had a lily with a snake wrapped around it. My symbol that the demons had claimed as a protective symbol, one to ward off danger.

Trey wrapped an arm around my shoulders and squeezed. "We thought you might like it."

"Was it Grandpa Rhys?" I asked.

"No, it was Trey," Mason answered before Trey could even open his mouth.

I looked up at Trey in shock. "You?"

He smiled softly, love seeping down our bond, and said, "Rhys and I have been working together, he's been training me in architecture and I've been learning from the various trades so that I could accomplish this for you. When I saw how sad the desolateness made you, I knew I had to do something. Something to see you smile just like this." He poked a corner of my mouth and smiled wide. "We have a lot more plans as well. Mason created a map from his flights over the land with Kayden's help and we're working with Jol and the Demon Council to develop the area in a way that allows the demons to thrive the best they can. Not like those of Jinla, but in a way that the demons need."

"Like leaving the mountainous areas alone, so Huk and the other giant demons have space to roam and hunt. We really want to ensure we don't hurt their food supplies," Kayden explained.

"We've also given the hellhounds a specific route so we can patrol the world to keep it safe and ensure we have all of our hunting grounds and breeding areas," Dhun said behind me.

I spun around with a smile for my friend and he pulled me away from Trey for a hug. "Dhun!"

"Hello, Lily."

I'd known Dhun had suggested that the hellhounds act as a patrolling force, but to hear that the routes had been established already *and* he had taken into account hunting and breeding showed how much Dhun had matured in such a short time.

"I can't believe you've all accomplished so much in such a short amount of time and without me knowing," I admitted. "What else have you done behind my back?"

"We also created a training facility so that we have our own protective force," Dhun answered.

"What?" I gasped.

"They're called the Demon Guard," Kora said in a really excited high-pitched voice. "They'll protect us from invaders."

Wow. They really had been doing a lot without me realizing it. To be fair, I'd been really focused on my training and the orphanage for the past month.

I hugged each of them, including the kids, and smiled at my family. "Thank you all. Seriously, this makes me so happy to hear and to see. I can't wait to see how much we can improve the lives here and how well the demons will thrive."

"Princess!" Zoman called as he ran towards us, a hand in the air.

"Hello, Zoman," I greeted.

"I've been looking for you," he advised and ran a hand through his hair, between his horns, smoothing down the wild locks. "The farmers are asking for you to visit the crops again. The field on the east side."

"Oh? Is something wrong?" I asked and immediately started heading in that direction. Mason and Kayden flanked me while Trey picked up Elrith and Dhun picked up Kora to follow.

"You'll see," he said cryptically.

"How goes your search for a mate?" I asked with a sideways glance at him as we walked.

His cheeks flushed, and he looked away from me. "Fine."

"Oh ho! Did you find someone you fancy already?" I asked, trying and failing to hide my smile.

"I won't jinx it by discussing it," he replied immediately. "Anyway, how did you like the housing development? Trey spent a lot of time on that."

Glancing over my shoulder at my mate, I said, "I love it. I can't wait for us to have enough housing that the demons won't have to worry about it in the future."

"Your father, er, the striped-haired one, suggested we develop a curriculum to teach constructions skills to demons who want to learn, so that we can build the houses in the future instead of requiring bringing people from the other world. I hear that there are many males eager to sign up here."

The striped-haired one? Oh, he must have meant Triston, who was a tiger shifter.

"I think that's a great idea! I'm a little irritated I didn't think of it myself," I admitted.

As we approached the fields where they'd planted the crops, my eyes widened at the flourishing plots. The corn was already tall, much taller than if it was only being grown naturally. "Have the elves been coming to help often?"

"No," Zoman said and frowned at me. "Why do you ask?"

"The corn looks taller than it should be for how long it's been growing," I said.

"I know the elves commented on the quality of the soil, so perhaps it's that," he said and shrugged his shoulders.

There were several demons working in the fields, watering, picking weeds, and tending to the various crops. Some were picking the ripe fruits and vegetables and putting them in large containers that they then dumped into crates in a cart that sat nearby.

"So, what is it that they want me to do?" I asked.

"We'd like you to sing," Talrinir said from behind the cart as she straightened and dusted off her hands. "The plants always do better at the castle when you sing, so we thought it'd be a good test to see if it was because of your singing or something else."

"Oh. Okay. I can do that."

"If you'll just walk down the rows while singing, touch a

few of the plants, just like you do in the castle gardens, please."

"Any particular song request?"

"Mama, can we go play in the grass over there?" Elrith asked and pointed in the distance where a small hill was covered in green grass.

"As long as Kora and one of your fathers goes with you," I said with a nod.

"I'll go with you," Mason said. "I'm not tired and don't feel like being put to sleep by your mama again." He winked at me to let me know he was teasing before turning back to the kids. "Race you to the top of the hill?"

"One. Two. Three. Go!" Elrith shouted and Dhun, Kora, Elrith, and Mason took off towards the hill.

"The focus song would be good and any of those upbeat songs I think will do best," Talrinir said, answering my question.

"Very well, if I must," I said with a dramatic sigh.

She smiled and said, "We appreciate your sacrifice." Her smile slipped and she said, "Ah, sorry, that—"

I waved off her apology. "I know what you meant." Immediately, I started down the first row and began singing, arms out so I could touch the leaves of the plants as I went. The farmers smiled and bowed to me when I passed them and I smiled and waved in return, but kept up my singing. It took five songs for me to finish my path down all of the rows of crops, but when I finished and returned to Zoman, Talrinir, Trey, and Kayden, they were staring in wonder at the crops.

"What?" I asked as I turned back to look, trying to see what they saw. Then, I saw it. The crops were all glowing a slight silver in color now, like they were ... sparkling.

"How interesting," Trey whispered. "The plants have never glowed in the castle gardens."

"Nor the ones at home," Kayden commented.

"I swear, it's like I keep finding out new abilities or unlocking new ones now that we're staying here in the demon world," I whispered as I stared in awe at the plants.

"It's going to be interesting to see what you can do in a year," Zoman said and Talrinir nodded with a huge smile, her doglike ears flopping back and forth in her excitement.

A flying demon with leathery wings headed our way and we all looked up at it.

"That isn't a good sign," Zoman growled and drew his sword.

"What?" I asked.

"They usually fly in packs," Talrinir explained. "And like to set things on fire."

"Trey," I snapped.

He immediately shifted into his dragon form. Without a moment's hesitation, he flew up into the sky and roared at the flying demon, trying to scare it off.

A few moments later, ten more of them appeared, all headed in the same direction.

"Does this happen often?" I asked as I watched Trey bump his head into the flying demon, trying to veer its flight path.

"We have occasional attacks, maybe once a week," one of

the farmers, a male demon with hooves and a set of thin, but long horns atop his head. "Usually foraging demons who want food. We don't often have just straight attacks, but those ..." he pointed at them. "... they like to destroy things."

"We should give them somewhere they can go to destroy things," I suggested.

"What?" Zoman asked.

"Give them an area of do what they want. If it's in their nature, it's not fair of us to deny them that. We should embrace it and help them find a place to do what comes natural to them."

"What about the mountains on the far side?" Mason suggested. "I remember seeing some trees there that regrow pretty quickly. If we can replant them quickly, then they could return there, burn them when they want, and leave the crops alone."

"We'll have to try it soon," I said. "I'd hate to kill them just because they're following their instincts."

"We should ask Huk to speak to them," Talrinir said.

We all turned to her. "What?" I asked. "He can speak to them?"

She nodded. "He might also know of the best spots for them to go burn things since he wanders the mountains the most. I'll talk to him tomorrow about it. We're scheduled to meet him at the orphanage for more discussions."

"Thank you, Talrinir." I smiled at her and said, "You're really good at this, you know?"

"At what?" she asked, blushing slightly.

"Ruling."

She sputtered and turned away. "I'm not *ruling*, I'm helping solve issues."

"That's exactly what a ruler does," Trey said with a soft chuckle.

"Whatever," she muttered.

CHAPTER
TWENTY-FOUR

Kayden kept his hands over my eyes as he directed me from my room, through the house, and out the back door. Trey trailed us, while Mason stayed in the other room to deal with the kids.

"Kay, if it's a dead animal again, I'm going to be mad," I said.

He sighed. "I only did that once when I was six. You were sick and wouldn't eat, so I thought if I brought you a snack that it'd help."

"It was twice and both times I told you not to do it again." Truthfully, young me had really appreciated the gesture and thoughtfulness.

"It's not a dead animal," he snapped and exhaled harshly through his nose.

"He put a lot more thought into this gift," Trey reassured me.

"Well, I guess if Trey is vouching for you..."

Kayden growled, making me smile victoriously. It was so easy getting him riled up.

The sound of bubbling water reached my ears, and I immediately scowled. We didn't have water running here, no stream or fountain or anything was near us.

Wait! Had he built a fountain for me?

Or a pool I could soak in in my snake form?

I did miss the pool my parents had built for me.

Kayden removed his hands from my eyes, and I squealed in delight.

"A spa! How did you manage this?"

"I had a little help," he admitted sheepishly.

Looking around the vicinity, I realized it was so much more than a spa. He had built an oasis for me.

There was a spa with rocks built around it, a pool with a waterfall and cave, as well as an adorable gazebo with vines starting to grow up the base of each corner. They had even built a privacy fence around the back yard.

"It's ... amazing," I breathed out and threw my arms around his neck before kissing him deeply. Pulling back, I rested my hand on his cheek and asked, "How did you do it? Even with magic you would need to dig the holes and move it all."

"You didn't notice that we've been leaving only through the front door for the past two weeks and that there's been a magical barrier up to keep the construction noise in for the past week? It was actually way too easy to get this done," Kayden teased.

"Well, what are we waiting for?" Trey asked, pulled his shirt off, and jumped into the pool.

Smiling, I followed suit, now understanding why they'd dressed me while I'd remained blind, since they'd put my swimsuit on.

I stood on the edge of the water, admiring my handsome and muscular mate. I was one lucky woman.

"Like the view?" Trey asked.

Nodding, I said, "I love it."

Kayden tugged his shirt off and jumped in next with his arms wrapped around his legs in a cannonball, sending a tidal wave of water at Trey. Kayden focused on me as he surfaced, a small smile on his face. "You really like it?"

I jumped in, barely making a splash, but swam to Kayden. "I love it, Kay. It's the perfect little oasis for us. Now, I can come soak in the water in my snake form whenever I want, and we can soak in the hot tub; and get a babysitter, so we can also break it in."

He captured my lips with his, his tongue thrusting into my mouth as his lust surged down our bond and I felt him grow hard against my stomach. "Temptress," he breathed out before nipping my neck playfully.

"Pool!" Elrith shouted as he and Kora ran out towards us with brightly colored, inflated, plastic rings around their stomachs. They jumped in on either side of me, splashing me with water.

Mason followed next, his shirt gone and only a pair of swim shorts on. "They barely waited long enough for me to inflate the floatation devices, despite knowing neither of them can swim well."

Elrith kicked his feet wildly to propel himself into the

center, next to Trey. "I've never been in a pool before! It was just too exciting."

"I can swim, a bit, but these make it so much easier," Kora noted as she set her hand atop her inflated ring with ducks decorating it.

Kayden swam over to the far side of the pool, where a square, container sat, pulled out several pool noodles, and tossed them to us. "Pool fight!" he yelled.

I quickly grabbed one and bopped Trey on the head with it, earning a wide-eyed, shocked expression from my usually stoic, dragon shifter mate.

"Wow, to be betrayed so quickly," he gasped and immediately bopped me back.

"No!" Elrith yelled and swung his pool noodle at Trey, who dodged it easily. "No one attacks my mama without suffering the reper... er... my wrath!"

"Ah!" Kora yelled as she ganged up on Trey with Elrith, always helping him to defeat whatever foe he faced.

"Everyone, get Trey!" I ordered and waved my floppy pool noodle towards him.

Trey dove under the water and kicked to propel himself away, towards safety, but Mason grabbed his foot, halting his progress.

We played until the sun set and our fingers were beyond wrinkly, but it was so worth it for all of the smiles and laughter.

After a shower and change of clothes, we sat at the small table in the gazebo and ate dinner, enjoying the waterfall sounds and peaceful night.

"I like it here," Kora whispered around her food.

"That makes me happy to hear," Kayden said, genuine joy filling our bond.

"I meant here, with you all," she admitted, "but here, in this area is nice, too."

"I have the best family," Elrith said with a nod, but then his lips turned down. "Sometimes, I miss my family, though."

Setting my hand atop his on the table, I smiled sadly and said, "That's perfectly normal and okay. I miss my dad, too, what little I remember of him. My adoptive parents are incredible, but there's something you can't replace with blood family at times. Though, I think found family is great."

"My parents are good," Kora said, "but there's a lot of fighting amongst the hounds and against other demons. It's nice to be somewhere safer and quieter. Nights were always chaotic in the wilderness. There were demons that hunted us and so many sounds."

Trey set his hand on her head and said, "You're very brave, Kora."

She smiled up at him. "I know. Dad says I'm the bravest pup."

"Once things settle down more in the other world, I want to take them to visit the werewolves," I informed my mates. "Papa Dan will love them."

"Why not invite him here? He's not king anymore and I know he misses you," Mason suggested. "We could invite all your family for a housewarming of sorts."

My eyes widened. Mason, the brooding, angry ball of wrath had just suggested a housewarming party. I looked up at the sky, but it was still solid, not falling apart.

"Rude," Mason said with narrowed eyes.

"What?" I asked.

"I heard you say the sky wasn't falling apart, suggesting it has to be the end of the world for me to say we should have a party," he said.

"Wait!" I gasped and jumped to my feet. "You *heard* me? Does that mean our bond is working, finally?"

"I heard it, too," Trey admitted and looked down at Kora. "Did she not say that out loud?"

"She looked up, but didn't talk," Kora said with a frown. "What are you talking about?"

"Mates are supposed to communicate telepathically when close together once they've formed a bond," I inform her. "Well, most can. We've not been able to. I thought it was because we're a mixed group, but there are others without the issue, so we've been uncertain why."

"Telepath... huh?" she tilted her head to the side, reminding me of her canine form.

"In our minds," I explained and tapped my temple.

"Oh! Like Dad does with me!" she realized and smiled.

"Yes," I agreed.

"Try to say something else," Mason urged me.

"*I want a tattoo,*" I thought mentally while looking at the snake he had on his chest.

"We can get matching tattoos if you want," he said aloud, and then a huge smile split his face. "Wait, let me try."

There was silence a moment and then...

"*Trey should get a tattoo, too.*"

Kayden and Mason high-fived in excitement and it was such a childish thing for them to do, so reminiscent of our group growing up together, that I burst into laughter and tears of joy streamed down my face.

"*Well, that's one less problem we have to worry about,*" Trey said mentally.

"I don't think I like you talking without us hearing," Elrith commented. "What if you're saying things we need to hear?"

"Like where we hid the cookies?" I teased.

He gasped. "I *knew* you'd hidden them!"

"First one to find them gets *two* cookies!" Kayden said and stood quickly.

Kora and Elrith yipped in excitement and ran back into the house, the goal to find the cookies before Kayden did.

"I'm really glad we are able to use it now," Mason admitted. "That way you can tell us when you're being attacked or when you need something."

"Let's hope I don't get attacked anytime soon," I said with a longing sigh. "Let's hope this next year is a little more peaceful than this previous one."

"I feel like we brought you a ton of danger when we returned home," Trey said with a frown and stabbed at his pasta a little harder than he'd been.

"While I don't believe in pre-determined lives, I do believe in fate a bit, and you three are definitely fated for me," I said with a smile. "I knew it when I was a kid, and I know it for certain now. I think even if you'd not returned for my birthday that we would have ended up seeing each other and we'd have been together shortly thereafter anyway." I tapped the necklace, no longer a tool of the Grand Advisor and now mine. "This was destined for me from my ancestor."

"I think it's been helping you heal," Mason said. "It glows while you're sleeping from time to time, like it's helping rejuvenate you."

My eyes widened. "Really?" I glanced down at the necklace and wondered what else it could do. Third to Reign had possessed a lot of abilities and if she'd seen me coming, perhaps she'd spelled it for more than we knew.

"I worried someone was using it again, but the feeling from it wasn't a bad one, it was more like ... warmth, so I didn't think it was necessary to bring it up. Plus, you always looked better after it did it." Mason shrugged. "Seems like I might be right."

"Your ancestors are very interesting," Trey said and smiled at me. "Makes sense, since you're incredibly intriguing as well."

"Intriguing, huh?" I teased and leaned forward, letting him get a nice view of my cleavage across the table. "Is that all I am, mate?"

He growled softly. "I love it when you use that word."

"Found 'em!" Elrith yelled victoriously.

"Save one for me!" I yelled back, winked at Trey, and ran into the house to join the kids for dessert.

TWENTY-FIVE

"Where are the napkins?" I shouted as I ran around the kitchen, trying to find the stack of napkins I had taken out just a minute ago. I swore I'd put them on the island, but now they were gone!

"On the end of the table, at the end of the buffet line, so it will be the last thing they pick up," Kayden answered from behind me before wrapping his arms around me. "Take a deep breath, Lily."

I obeyed, taking a deep breath in before slowly letting it out. "I just want everything to be perfect."

"Your family are coming to see you," he whispered in my ear, his breath hot on the shell of it, making me shiver and arch back more into him. "Yes, they want to see this place, but you're what is important to them. We could be in a tent and they wouldn't care." He chuckled. "Well, they'd want to build you something nicer than a tent if that's what they found us living in, but you know what I mean."

I turned around and kissed him gently on the lips. "Thank you."

He rubbed the tip of his nose against mine, something we used to do when younger. "Anytime. Now, go to your room and change while your mates finish setting up down here." He swatted my butt and pushed my shoulders to direct me down the hallway.

On my way to my room, I popped my head into Elrith's room, smiling when I found him and Kora playing with blocks that Dad had found in our storage that used to be mine when I was their age. They'd built what looked like the layout of a city, very similar in shape to Obselk. "You guys ready to meet more of my family?" I asked.

Kora looked up, a little fear in her eyes. "Will they like me?"

Squatting down, I met her eyes and nodded. "They'll love you. My Papa Dan, especially, will like you."

"How do you know?" she asked softly. "I'm a demon and they aren't."

"I'm a demon, too, and they love me. Plus, Papa Dan loves me a ton and you're a lot like me."

"I am?" she gasped.

"Yes," I nodded. "You're a lot like me when I was your age." I actually worried it might make him cry and get senti-mental, but it was hard to tell with him sometimes. Though, Grandpa Deryn swears he's getting more sentimental the older he gets.

She smiled and stood. "I'm going to wear one of my new dresses."

I stood as well and said, "That sounds like a great idea, Kora."

"I'll wear my new shirt!" Elrith said. "The one Grandpa Triston got me."

"I think he'll like that," I agreed. "I'm going to change now, okay?"

They nodded, already headed in different directions to get their clothes.

There were still a couple hours until my family was scheduled to arrive, so I hopped in the shower, allowing myself time to decompress and relax a bit. I knew Kayden was right, but my bigger anxiousness came from it being my first time hosting my grandparents and great grandparents. I'd helped Mom and Dad, but this was my first time as the hostess.

After showering, brushing out my hair, and putting on some light makeup, I stood in my closet and debated which dress to wear.

"The purple one," Mason said behind me.

I hissed in shock as I spun around, glaring at him as I felt his joy at startling me. "Rude, Mason. Rude."

"You're so easy to startle and make the cutest little hisses," he teased as he wrapped me in a hug and bit my neck.

Gasping and arching into him, I gripped his shirt and said, "You bite me again and we won't make it to the party."

"Promise?" he breathed against my neck, his breath warm against the wet spot from his bite.

With every ounce of willpower I could muster, I shoved him gently away. "Out."

He pouted, reminding me of his ten-year-old self when I'd refused to let him steal one of my shiny pens. "Fine."

Once I was certain he was on his way out, I turned back to the closet and pulled the purple dress off the hanger. The dress was made from silk from a small bug-like demon that reminded me of a silkworm back in the other world, but so much softer. It was easy to spell with designs, too, which Druth apparently loved making. She designed this dress for me and did all the spell work herself, spending three days on it, according to Azgon. The vibrant purple matched the purple within my hair when it glowed and had a series of flowers and vines made from tiny crystals around the edges and around the mermaid cut bodice. There were slits on each side of the dress, but since it overlaid a bit, you only noticed if I stretched my leg out. It was the perfect style for someone who might need to fight while wearing it, which was a testament to my life so far that I needed that.

The only issue I had with the dress was that it was impossible to put on alone because you had to tie the laces in the back.

"Mason!" I called.

"Yes?" he asked, right behind me ... again.

I couldn't stop the hiss before it came out, which made him chuckle.

His warm fingertips slid down my bare shoulders to the laces. "Need help with these?"

"Yes, please." I nodded.

"Oh, being polite today, are we? How refreshing."

I rolled my eyes. "I'm always polite."

He scoffed and began tightening the laces carefully. "Often, not always."

"Pot. Kettle."

His lips pressed against one shoulder and then the next. "Guilty."

"Is everything ready?" I asked when he finally finished tightening the laces and patted my back to let me know.

"Yes. The kids are dressed and Kora even let me braid her hair," he announced.

My mouth dropped. "*You* braided her hair?"

His mouth curved down into a frown. "I'm great at braiding hair."

"You braided mine into knots," I reminded him.

"That was on purpose because you were being mean to me that day." He smiled and said, "I actually watched a lot of videos on how to properly braid, in case you ever asked me to."

"Can you braid tight to the side of my head?" I asked, curious.

He nodded. "Yes." His eyes dropped to the dress and then up to my hair. "It would actually look really good with this dress. Want me to show you?"

Glancing at the clock on the wall, I hesitated because it was near time.

"Sit on the edge of the bed. We have enough time."

I was careful with the dress as I sat and despite my nervousness about the time, I really wanted to see what he could do.

"I even made Kayden let me practice on him when he had long hair," Mason admitted.

"Wait? When did Kay have long hair?"

"He grew it out for about a year," Mason explained as he began to braid my hair on the right side of my head. "When we decided to come home to see you, though, he cut it."

"Did it look bad?" I asked. Kayden would look good in any hairstyle, I thought.

"No, but he wanted to look his best when we saw you again, so he opted for a cut that he could style." He paused and sighed loudly.

"What?"

"I forgot to grab hair bands first."

Standing, he held the hair he had finished braiding as we walked to the bathroom together to get the small rubber bands I kept for the rare occasions when I braided my hair.

I froze as I stared at the mirror and the beautiful braid along the right side of my head above my ear. It was incredibly well done and showed he had indeed practiced a lot.

"You like it so far?" he asked, nervousness flitting down our bond.

"It's amazing," I praised. Looking in the mirror to meet his eyes, I asked, "You really learned this for me?"

He wrapped an arm around my waist and rested his chin atop my head, our eyes locked in the mirror. "I knew you were the one for me when I was a child and that never left. The separation we experienced was agonizing and I know we've discussed wishing we could go back and change it, but throughout it all, I never stopped preparing to be your mate. I never stopped doing what I could to become someone that would be useful to you. Whether that use came from my blade or my hands, I made certain I was preparing."

Tears pooled in my eyes, but I blinked them away quickly so I didn't ruin my makeup. "I love you so much, Mason."

He kissed the top of my head and smiled at me in the mirror. "I love you, too. Now, let's get this braiding job finished before your family shows up."

When he did finish, I couldn't believe how gorgeous it looked and how well it fit with the dress like he'd said it would.

There was a press of magic just as we headed out of the bedroom and I heard Mom squeal the next moment, which told me she and my fathers had teleported in.

"That dress looks even better on you than I thought it would," Mom praised Kora.

We stepped into the living room and watched as Kora did a spin in it. "I like when it flies out!" Kora announced.

Mom gushed over her and it warmed my heart so much because I knew she would have reacted the exact same way had Kora been my blood related child or not. She was just an amazing person and knew these children deserved love.

Triston high-fived Elrith over his shirt choice and I was happy to see them bonding more.

Riddick noticed me first and whistled. "Where did our little girl go?" He walked over and hugged me, pushing Mason away with a hand to his chest. "You get her whenever you want. Let us have some time."

"You've been saying that since I was eight," I teased.

Branson pulled me away from Riddick and hugged me, patting my head gently. "And it's truer now." Pushing me back, he asked, "Who braided your hair? It definitely wasn't you."

I stuck my tongue out at him. "Actually, Mason did it."

Branson looked over my head at Mason and said, "Maybe you're alright for Lily after all. Any warrior who learns to braid for their mate is good in my book."

"Thanks for the approval," Mason grumbled sarcastically, but I could feel his genuine joy in our bond. Boys were so silly with their emotions sometimes.

Caleb grabbed me and draped an arm around my shoulders. "Show me around your new place before your grandparents get here."

"Too late," Grandpa Nico said behind us.

"I can show everyone around," I told Dad and gave him a quick hug before I turned to face part of my family.

Grandpa Nico, Deryn, Rhys, and Foxfire stood behind Nana Jolie, all of them holding packages. "We brought presents," Nana Jolie announced.

"For who?" I asked with an arched brow.

She laughed. "All of you, actually. Mason, take the one Deryn has. Kayden, take the one Rhys has. Elrith and Trey, I have yours. Kora, take the one from Nico. Lily, take the one from Foxfire."

Trey, Mason, and I stared at her in shock, unmoving.

She smiled and said, "Well, I've had some gifts for you for a bit, but keep missing my chance to give them to you. So, I figured now is the best time. Come on, get your presents and open them."

It wasn't a holiday, but I wasn't going to say no to presents.

"Go on," I urged the kids, and they moved to get their presents.

My present was a new bracelet with several small mana stones in it full of magic. "There's a bit from each of us," Grandpa Foxfire explained. "We wanted you to have a bit of each of us with you. Just in case." He pulled me into a hug and whispered, "I had to restrain your grandmother when we heard you were attacked. She wanted to burn everything down to get to you. We know you're an adult now and capable of handling yourself and that you're happy here, but we still worry for you."

"Thank you, Grandpa."

"I'm going to pick up your great grandparents. I'll be right back," Grandpa Nico said and disappeared the next instant.

I watched the kids excited over the new toys they'd been given. "Take them to your room, please," I ordered them.

My mates had received some new videogames, ones that you didn't need internet to play, which was nice since we did not yet have internet in the demon world. I knew the guys were missing playing games, so this would help. We'd also been given some new board games and card games, which would be great for family game nights.

"How did you like the bathroom?" Grandpa Rhys asked with a wide smile.

I hugged him and said, "Thank you so much. It's amazing. Honestly, once I'm in there it is hard to leave."

He laughed and smiled happily at my compliment. "I knew you'd need a space for decompressing."

"Wait until you see the oasis in the backyard," I informed him.

His eyes widened. "What?"

"You have to wait until everyone is here," Trey said. "So we can give one tour."

"Sounds like you're just being lazy," Nana Jolie teased him.

"Efficient, not lazy," he said with a smile.

She scoffed. "You dragons are so alike."

"Hey!" Grandpa Rhys said, indignant.

"Where's my favorite great granddaughter?" Papa Dan yelled as soon as he was teleported in.

I rushed over and hugged the large werewolf around his stomach since that was as high as I could reach. "Papa!"

He hugged me tight. "There you are, pup!" After a tight squeeze he pushed me back and stared down into my eyes, emotion swirling in his. "Can you please be more careful moving forward? I don't like hearing that you were injured."

I smiled and said, "I will be more careful, promise."

He frowned. "Your dad said the same thing before and ended up getting captured a few times since that promise. So, that's not too reassuring. Maybe I need to move here with you, so I can be closer in case of emergency and in case you need a babysitter."

I laughed, but then realized he was serious. "You want to move here? With us in the demon world?"

He patted my back. "We'll talk later, but since I'm retired now, I've got time on my hands and I'd like to spend more time with those two pups." He tilted his head towards Elrith and Kora who were chatting with my grandparents, telling them a story about something I couldn't hear. "I can get my construction team to build a separate house, I don't intend to impose on yours, but if your king is amenable to it, I'd like to move here."

"I'd love to have you around more," I replied immediately and meant it.

"We all would," Kayden said behind me.

Papa Dan pulled Kayden into a hug. "How you doin', Kay?"

"Better now that Lily's recuperating here," he replied.

"She does look better," Papa Dan agreed, and they both looked at me.

"You sure you don't want to move her for a change of pace and a bit of newness?" Mason asked.

Papa Dan smiled. "That is part of it. I won't lie about a change of scenery being in order for this old man."

"Sorry we're late!" Tony yelled as he came in through the front door with Maya, elf Tony, and Jaeden right behind him.

"Maya!" I yelled and raced over to hug my friend.

We both squealed and hugged each other tightly, holding onto each other longer than usual since it'd been so long since we'd seen each other.

"What am I, chopped liver?" my brother asked with a scoff.

I patted his shoulder while still hugging Maya. "Thanks for coming, bro."

Mason walked over and hugged Tony. "Don't mind her, she's just been needing some Maya time lately."

"I don't know how I feel about all of you together," Dad said. "Whenever you lot are together, craziness happens."

"Well, don't start the party without me," Piper said as she joined us, Talrinir behind her.

I hugged each of them. "Thanks for bringing her, Talrinir."

Talrinir smiled. "Anything for you, friend."

"Would you like to stay?" I offered.

"No, you spend time with your family. You and I will catch up in two days at our next meeting." She hugged me again before heading out the door.

"Tell Jol I said hi," I teased her.

She flushed and stuck her tongue out at me when she realized I was teasing.

"Alright, everyone is here, give us the tour now," Dad ordered.

"Yes, sir," I replied, but it was Trey who led the tour.

I followed at the back, watching as my adoptive family, friends, and the kids all chatted, smiled, and laughed together.

This was what all of the fighting and pain had been for.

This moment of complete peace and joy.

It made it all worth it.

"So, I've been thinking," Grandpa Rhys whispered to me as everyone walked around and inspected the backyard, praising Kayden on his work.

"Oh?" I asked. "Should I be scared or intrigued?"

He chuckled. "Both."

I waited for him to elaborate.

"I'd like to build a compound of houses here for our family. I know we'll need Jol's blessing, but I know all of us would like to visit more frequently, and we don't want to impose in your house, especially with how many of us there are. Plus, I overheard Dan talking about moving here, and I think that's a great idea for the old wolf. He's been bored lately and missing you."

"I would love that," I said. "And I know Jol won't have an issue with it."

He smiled. "Great! It'll make visiting for holidays much easier." His smile dropped and I didn't realize it was because I'd started crying until he wiped one from my cheek. "What?"

"I'm just so thankful that you all are so accepting of me, of us," I indicated Elrith and Kora and the world beyond.

He hugged me and patted my back. "My sweet granddaughter, you could be an alien and I'd still love you."

"You're making my mate cry again?" Trey growled and pulled me away from Grandpa Rhys to wipe his thumbs beneath my eyes, likely fixing my mascara. "Do I need to fight him?"

I smiled. "Not this time. These are happy tears."

"You think you could take me? I think you're still a decade away at least," Grandpa Rhys teased.

"I could, but that might make my mate sad, so I won't," Trey replied nonchalantly.

"Actually, I am curious how much stronger you've become," Dad said. "I think we should have some training sessions tomorrow."

"I want to train, too!" Elrith yelled.

"Me, too!" Kora yelled, raised her hand, and bounced on the balls of her feet, causing her dress to bounce with her adorably.

"It's been a while since I've had a chance to go against you," Mason said to Dad. "I think I can take you this time."

Dad smiled wide. "Sounds fun."

"Tomorrow at noon at our house," Nana Jolie said. "We'll have snacks, drinks, and fun!"

"Actually, I'd like to test something with you and Lily here," Trey said. "It seems that she has what resembles siren powers here, and I'd like to see if you can be affected by it."

"Oh, how interesting!" Nana Jolie said and smiled at me. "Leona is going to be even more sad they weren't able to attend tonight once she hears about this."

"I'm sure she'll be here to visit soon enough," Trey said. "We know she and Silverowl like to check up on Lily as much as you do."

"We're family, that's what family does," Nana Jolie said and winked at me.

We all went inside to eat and spend time together. It was an evening full of laughs and love. Exactly what I'd hoped it would be.

Mom draped her arm around my shoulders and pulled me into her side where I stood at the edge of the living room watching it all. "You've done well, Lily. I'm so proud of you. You've become an amazing woman and I know you're going to accomplish even more with all of the plans you have for the orphans of both worlds and the unification as well. Just remember, you're not alone and we'll be here to help you whenever you need it."

I leaned my head on her shoulder and said, "Thank you, Mama. For everything. If you hadn't adopted me ... I'm not sure what would have happened."

She looked over at my mates who were bickering with my fathers about something. "Those men were made for you, just like mine were made for me. Fate has always had a way of sticking us in the path of the ones we're meant to be with. And while I know I can never be your birth mom, I'm so glad I was able to become a part of your life. I've never once regretted picking you up that day and taking you home. Just like I know you'll never regret it with Elrith. He and Kora are a lot like you. Strong, powerful, and determined to prove to the world that there's more to them than their uniqueness. It's going to be an interesting next decade."

Glancing over at Maya and her group of men, I said, "I can't wait to see that develop more."

Mom laughed softly. "Your brother is smitten for sure. He may not have wanted to admit it before, but that group works well together. These next generations are really going to be something."

While we hadn't eradicated the new hate group, I knew it was only a matter of time. With my family working together, integrating themselves in both worlds and working to improve the lives of all races, I knew everything would be alright.

No matter what hardships we faced. No matter what new issues arose. This family would stay strong, work together, and our bonds would only deepen.

My mates looked at me, and I felt their love through our bond. This was my happily ever after and I would continue to work hard, to learn more, to improve, to ensure that nothing jeopardized it in the future.

"Who's ready for dessert?" I announced.

"Me!" Kora, Elrith, Grandpa Foxfire, and Papa Dan yelled simultaneously.

"Ah, yes, all the children," Nana Jolie teased, earning laughter from everyone.

Yes, this was exactly what life was supposed to be. Found family loving and laughing together.

EPILOGUE

12 YEARS LATER

"Auntie!" Kora yelled, spotting me first. Her hair and the quills within her hair bounced against her back as she raced towards me.

Elrith's eyes snapped up from the phone he'd been looking down at, at her exclamation. "Mama!" he shouted, a huge smile splitting his teenage face. He'd grown a lot since we first met him over a decade ago. No longer did he have the baby chub on his cheeks. Now, he was lean and muscular with great control over his shifting, to the point that he currently looked human, except for the horns on his head.

I opened my arms and braced myself as they both ran into me, squeezing me for all they could, which I could thankfully withstand. I, however, had to restrain myself since I could crush them if I squeezed too hard. "My babies!" I crooned. "Did you miss me?"

Elrith looked down at me, now over six feet tall, and nodded. "So much. I love Nana Jolie and my grandpas, but it's not the same as living with you and my papas." He frowned and looked over my head. "Are you alone? Mama! You can't be alone, even now."

"I'll protect you, Auntie," Kora assured me, spinning around to survey our surroundings for threats.

Chuckling softly, I patted them both on the heads, a reach for Elrith. "Calm down, imps. You really think my overprotective mates would let me come here alone?"

Mason flew down from a nearby tree in his crow form, shifting into his man form as he neared us. "Of course we wouldn't. We were just letting her have her reunion with you before we came in." He took turns hugging the kids and patted Kora on her head. "I heard you saved Elrith again."

Elrith scoffed. "I had my scales up. The arrow wouldn't have even pierced my skin or hurt me at all."

"Only because I grabbed it out of the air before it could touch you," Kora said, and beamed proudly.

Even though we'd eradicated the group that had formed with the sole intent of killing demons and preventing them from coming to this world, there were still threats and those who didn't like the demons being here.

Elrith, being Prince of Demons and Hybrids was a prime target for them. Thankfully, the little imp turned out to be very strong and never missed a training session. He spent his evenings while in this world training with Grandpas Rhys, Nico, Foxfire, and Deryn, or my adoptive fathers, and when in our home in the demon world, he spent evenings training with Great Grandpa Dan.

When Papa Dan had asked to move to the demon world, I had been shocked, but it had turned out to be the ultimate blessing. He trained the kids, helped watch them when we wanted to go on dates or had issues to attend to, and he'd even adopted a couple teenage orphans.

"Are you ready to head home?" I asked. "Kayden is preparing something delicious for our return."

"We need to grab our bags from Grandma Ember's house," Kora said. "We stayed there this week because Nana and Grandpas had a videogame tournament."

A huge smile split my face as I remembered that my great grandmother and her mates were participating in the newest fighting videogame's tournament circuit. Their team was dominating and it was one of the rare instances where they could do something they loved and where it didn't matter that they were royals, since it was all based on skill. I wasn't as good as Nana Jolie, but my mates and I were improving. It had become a family battle, to see which pack could defeat them. My brother, Tony, Maya, Tony the elf, and Jaeden were really good, too, and our current standings were six wins and six losses. Tomorrow, we would secure another win for sure to beat them.

"That's perfect, since I know there are fresh baked snickerdoodle cookies at their house," Mason said and licked his lips hungrily. Bran Bran made the best snickerdoodles, so Mason wasn't the only one salivating at the idea of getting some to take home.

Elrith draped an arm around my shoulders and hugged

me against his side as we walked. "I missed you. How are you feeling? Any improvements?"

My shadow snake appeared and wrapped around his arm in a hug. "Yes, we're slowly getting better." About five years ago, my power to summon the shadows had returned, much to everyone's relief. I knew I didn't have what my biological grandmother, Third to Reign, had called Goddess Mode anymore, but having the shadows back was a huge relief.

Elrith laughed at the silly shadow snake who had a mind of her own far too often for being my power. "That's good to hear."

We climbed into the waiting SUV and Elrith leaned over to hug Trey who sat in the driver's seat.

"Where are we headed?" Trey asked.

"To my parents'," I announced as I buckled my belt.

"How's school going?" Trey asked the kids as he started driving.

"Math is killing me," Elrith admitted.

"I was invited to the advanced class and the debate team," Kora announced.

I gasped and spun in my seat to smile at her. "That's amazing! I bet your dad is super proud."

She nodded vigorously, her quills bouncing a bit. "He's coming to see me, us, tomorrow, and said he's bringing me a gift."

"Hopefully it's not another pup," Trey whispered.

I smacked his arm playfully. "Quiet, you."

"You love me like your own daughter, so hush," Kora said, and rolled her eyes.

She was completely correct. We loved her like a daughter, same as we loved Elrith as our son. Blood didn't matter to us, just like it hadn't my family.

As soon as we pulled through the gates of the hybrid lands, Mom ran out onto the porch.

I stepped out of the SUV and she immediately tackled me onto the grass, hugging me tightly. "My baby!"

Laughing, I hugged her back, not even caring that my tan pants definitely had grass streaks on them now. "Hi, Mom."

"Give me my daughter," Bran Bran growled and pulled me away from Mom.

She stuck out her bottom lip in a huge pout. "I never get time with her. You keep stealing her."

"Go hug the grandkids," Bran Bran grumbled against the top of my head as we both hugged each other as tightly as we could. After another second, he grunted and wheezed, "I give."

Chuckling, I loosened my grip. "Hi, Bran Bran."

He patted my cheek and said, "You look better and that grip has definitely returned."

"Where's –"

I didn't even get to finish my question before Dad pulled me away from Bran Bran to hug me. "My favorite daughter!" he crowed.

"I'm your only daughter," I reminded him.

"Potatoes, tomatoes," he growled.

"We can't stay long," Trey informed us. "Kayden has food ready."

"I just have to grab one thing," I said as I extricated myself from Dad's hold and slowly started backing up towards the house.

"Oh? And what is that?" Dad asked with a small smile.

Bran Bran turned, eyes narrowed, and asked, "Who told you?"

"Told me what, Bran Bran?" I asked with a sweet smile, continuing to back up. With a wink at Kora, who was at the porch next to me, I spun and darted into the house.

Bran Bran roared and I knew he was hot on my tail.

Calling on my shadow snake, I used her to trip Bran Bran, giving me time to make it to the kitchen, grab a plastic tub of snickerdoodles, and ran back out of the house.

"Thief!" Mom shouted and ran after me.

"Run, kids!" I shouted with a laugh. "Out run your grandparents or you won't get cookies."

Dad and Mom were neck and neck as they ran after me. Trey jogged lazily behind us, carrying the kids' bags, a happy smile on his face, which grew wider when Bran Bran tried to pass him and he tripped him.

Mason flew next to me, laughing his crow laugh.

Elrith ran by me, snatching the cookie tub out of my hands. "Too slow!"

I gasped. "Traitor!"

The hybrids milling around town watched us with smiles as we charged through, tripping and grabbing at each other to try to get the cookies and get to the demon portal.

At the portal stood a familiar, tall male demon, wings that had grown after fully accepting his mantle as king, folded behind his back.

"Jol!" I yelled. "Elrith has cookies!"

Jol's eyes focused on Elrith and the plastic container in

his hands. "Cookies? You must pay tribute to your king, Elrith."

Elrith stuck his tongue out at Jol and dodged the demon king. "Finders keepers."

Elrith darted through the portal with a victorious whoop.

"He's faster," Mom panted as she stopped next to me and pulled me into a one-armed hug.

"I think Dan's been giving him speed lessons," Dad grumbled.

"He's been training him a lot," I admitted. "Something about the hybrid king not getting any younger."

Dad growled and pushed me playfully. "I'm not that old yet."

"Not that young either," Mom teased.

He clutched his chest. "Even my own mate?"

She released me to hug him and kiss his cheek. "It's only facts, darling."

After a round of hugs, I went through the portal.

"Where's your mate?" I asked Jol.

"Too pregnant to be away from the castle," he answered. "Talrinir needs bedrest and the twins are with her now."

Jol and Talrinir had twins six years ago and she was pregnant once again with twins. The demons were all overjoyed at their king's family growing so much. We were as well.

"I can't wait to meet my new nieces or nephews," I said with a wide smile.

"Hey! You can't eat them yet!" Kora yelled.

I spun and gasped to find Elrith shoving a snickerdoodle into his mouth. "You close that container right now!"

Jol laughed and patted my back. "I'll contact you when the twins are born. Go deal with your imps."

"Tell Talrinir I said good luck," I called as I ran after Elrith, who was running away from Kora towards the house.

Mason and Trey ran on each side of me, both waving to demons as we passed them on our way.

Elrith threw open the door and yelled, "I'm home!"

Dan and Kayden looked up from the documents they'd been reviewing and smiled at us.

"Welcome home," Kayden called out as we all joined them.

Home. It was so nice to be home and have it filled with my family.

"Let's eat," Dan said as he pulled me into a hug. "I know this pup here is dying for a cookie."

"Elrith already snuck one," I said with a pout.

The wrinkles around the edges of Dan's eyes crinkled as he smiled. "Is that so? I guess that means he won't mind double training tonight, then? To work off those extra calories."

Elrith set the cookie container on the counter and said, "I'm going to win this time. Today is the day I defeat you."

"Good luck," Kayden said with a scoff and patted Elrith's shoulder. "Of all of us, only Lily and Mason have defeated Dan."

"I won, too," Kora said.

We all turned to look at her in disbelief.

"Yep, she defeated me last weekend," Dan replied. "I swear she used a speed enchantment or something."

"Just pure skill and talent," she said and flipped her hair

and quills over her shoulder, though I could see how happy she was to have defeated him.

"Maybe you're just getting slow?" I taunted.

"What to test it out?" he asked.

Laughing, I patted his shoulder. "No, thank you. I've retired from fighting. I'll leave it up to Elrith to defeat you."

"No more fighting for you," Mason grumbled and slid his arms around my waist from behind, hugging me back against his chest. "You just get pampered and loved."

"Come on, let's eat," Kayden ordered as he pulled out a dish from the oven.

We all sat around the dining table after saying bye to Dan. Looking at my little family, the freedom I had now, I couldn't have stopped myself from smiling even if I had wanted to.

It's good to be home. It's good to be loved. It's good to be their princess.

"I love you all," I said as I looked at the five of them.

Trey reached over and threaded his fingers with mine. "We know. We love you, too."

Elrith and Kora smiled at me and both suddenly announced, "We started courting!"

My jaw dropped. "What?"

Kora nudged Elrith, who cleared his throat awkwardly. "Well, Kora and I were talking and she agreed to let me court her, but then she found out that I'm not the only one she's connected to."

We had discovered on their sixteenth birthday that they were soulmates, a golden bond had formed between them, one they'd seen since they were kids, but hadn't known what it was. Then, much like what I'd done, Kora had used shadow powers to connect her and Elrith.

It shouldn't have been surprising that they were courting, they were seventeen, after all, with their eighteenth birthdays coming up in a few months.

"She's also being courted by two others," Elrith announced, though that wasn't as happy an announcement.

"Three," she corrected. "Turns out, I'm much like you, Auntie. I have four mates, though, not three."

"When do we get to meet them?" Mason asked, far too calmly for the protectiveness flowing through our bond from him.

"Tomorrow," she admitted with reddened cheeks. "They want to meet Dad and you all."

"Are they demons?" Trey asked.

Her cheeks were fully red now. "One is a hellhound with the ability to shift like me, he's a hybrid, his mom's an elf. The second is a hybrid from a dragon and a wolf. The last is ..." She paused before finishing, "... full demon."

"I'm happy for you, Kora. Just remember, you're the princess here, and those males need to convince you that you want to fully accept the bond. Make them prove their worth and show they're devoted to you. You don't have to accept just because there is a bond if they aren't ready for you."

"But be willing to forgive a time or two," Trey said and squeezed my hand. "Sometimes we make mistakes."

Looking at my three mates, it felt like a lifetime ago that we'd been separated by a misunderstanding. They were a part of me that I could never live without.

"Yes, remember to forgive, but only if they're actually repentant," I clarified with a wink at Trey.

"I think they shouldn't get a chance to court her unless they can defeat Mason," Elrith muttered.

"So, you can't court me either?" Kora asked with an arched brow.

He dropped his fork and gaped at her. "I defeated Mason."

"Once and while he wasn't at one hundred percent," Kora argued.

Elrith shoved his chair back as he stood. "Outside, now!" he ordered Mason.

Mason rolled his eyes. "You can wait until I finish eating."

Elrith scowled, but returned to his seat and food. "Fine, when you're done eating."

Holding in my laughter was hard, but I did allow myself to smile wide.

Life was never boring with this group, that was for sure, and I couldn't wait to see what the future had in store for my adopted children.

It was certain to be full of fun and challenges. With our family at their backs, though, they would defeat whatever they faced. Because that was what found family did. We supported each other no matter what, even if it meant letting your son challenge you to a duel to prove he was worthy of his soulmate.

I kissed Mason's cheek and whispered, "You better not go easy on him, you big softie."

He rolled his eyes at me, but didn't respond, since he knew I was right.

"Hey! Don't amp him up," Elrith growled.

"Don't growl at your mother," Trey ordered and pointed his fork at him.

Elrith pouted. "Sorry."

Yes, this family would be together no matter what the universe threw at us. Just as fate intended.

DON'T FORGET to join my newsletter: https://catbanks.co/ CB-Newsletter

If you enjoyed the series, please consider leaving a review! Looking for more reverse harem romance? Check out Their Fae Goddess, a complete reverse harem fae fantasy romance trilogy. books2read.com/QOTS

AFTERWORD

Thank you for joining me on this journey in the Her Royal Harem world! I hope you enjoyed this series as much as I enjoyed writing it.

Don't forget to check out my other books and tell your friends about this series.

I appreciate you taking the chance to read my books.

If you haven't yet, consider joining my newsletter where I host giveaways and share upcoming releases and information. https://catbanks.co/CB-Newsletter

Check out the awesome character art created of Lily by Covers by Juan and the other series characters by Grady Earls.

Lily

Trey

Mason

Kayden

Dhun as a puppy.

Chun as an adult.

King Jolmach

The Grand Advisor

CONNECT WITH CATHERINE BANKS

I really appreciate you reading my book! Here are some ways to connect with me:

www.catherinebanks.com

Join my newsletter for deals and snippets:

https://catbanks.co/CB-Newsletter

Buy directly from me at my shop at discounted prices: https://shop.catherinebanks.com

ABOUT THE AUTHOR

Catherine Banks is an award-winning, USA Today bestselling author who writes in several romance subgenres and has multiple pseudonyms. She began writing fiction at only four years old and finished her first full-length novel at the age of fifteen. She is married to her soulmate and best friend, Avery, who she has two amazing children with. After her full-time job, she reads books, plays video games, and watches anime shows and movies with her family to relax. Although she has lived in Northern California her entire life, she dreams of traveling around the world. Catherine is also C.E.O. of Turbo Kitten Industries™, a company with many hats including being a book publisher and store full of nerdy fun.

facebook.com/catherinebanksauthor
bookbub.com/authors/catherine-banks
amazon.com/author/catherinebanks